Murder at Solent Island Lighthouse

Book One – The Solent Island Mysteries

A Cozy Mystery

A. S. McClatchie

MURDER AT SOLENT ISLAND LIGHTHOUSE: COZY MYSTERY

Copyright © 2022 A. S. MCCLATCHIE

Print version © 2023 A. S. MCCLATCHIE

All rights reserved. This work may not be copied, duplicated, transmitted, broadcast or otherwise distributed in part or in the whole without the written permission of the author.

Murder at Solent Island Lighthouse is an original work of fiction that does not depict the actual names, circumstances, or events of individuals living or dead. Any similarity to such individuals or situations is entirely coincidental.

Published by April Showers Publishing

Dedicated to Linda and her love of mysteries.

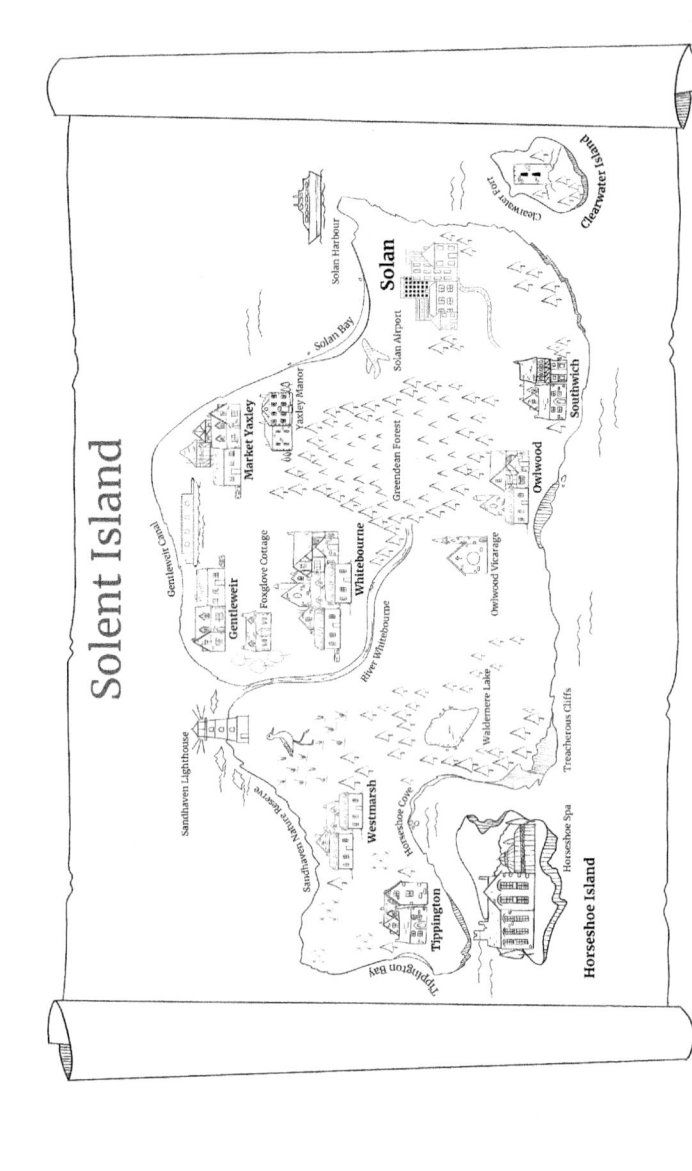

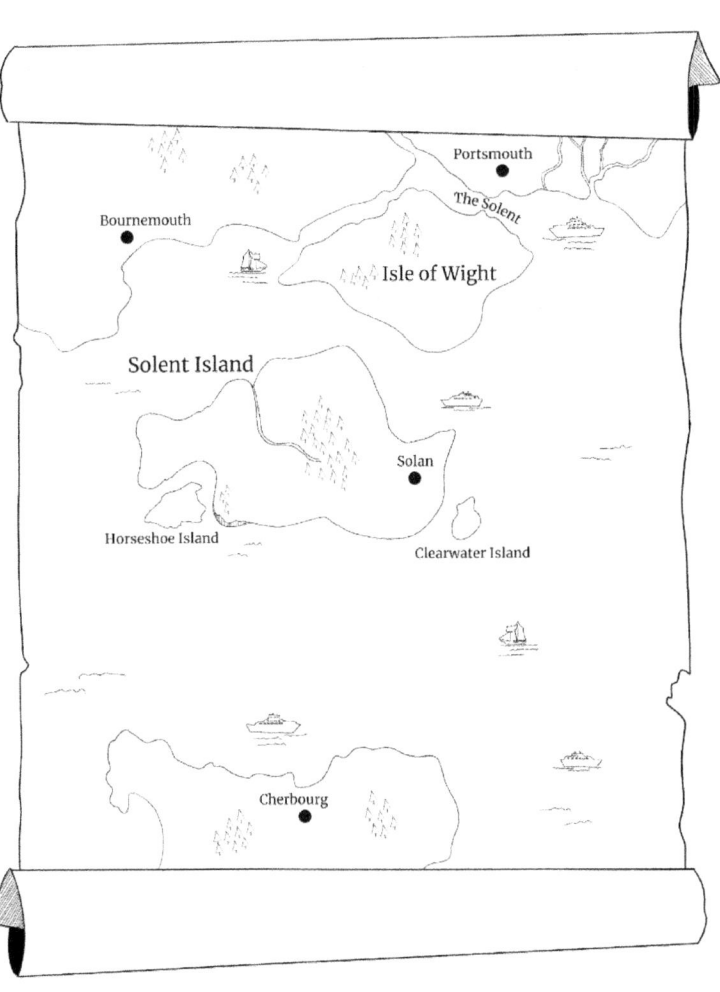

1

"Woah, woah, woah – where do you think you're going with that?" The contractor stopped Genny in her tracks as she tried to take a box of her belongings over the threshold.

Genny put down the box and stared at him for a few moments, confused.

"This is Foxglove Cottage, isn't it?" She asked gently. "I'm the new owner - I thought it was ready."

"Ah – you must be Mrs. Hadley-"

"-Ms."

"Ms. Hadley, my apologies," the contractor hastily corrected himself. "We spoke on the phone – I'm Mitchell Collins. My team are working flat out to get the cottage and adjoining bakery ready, but we won't be done until the 15th."

"No, no," Genny said, her voice rising in panic as she pulled her phone from her pocket to show him the email. "It says here the 5th!"

Mitchell peered at the phone through crinkled eyes and his face fell, "I'm sorry, that must be a typo. My thumbs are too big, I'm always doing that. Half my crew are still up at the lighthouse on the cliffs in Westmarsh so work will be faster once they join us."

Dread flooded Genny as she surveyed the man in front of her, swallowing down words of frustration. He wasn't unsympathetic, one hand in the pocket of his dust-coated jeans, and the other running through salt and pepper hair with a regretful motion.

This had all been a big misunderstanding.

"Mr. Collins-"

"Call me Mitchell-"

"-Mitchell. I've just gotten off of a ferry from the mainland after selling my London flat, boxing up everything I owned and saying goodbye to my loved ones who are now hundreds of miles away. Is there nothing you can do to help me get into my new home tonight?"

"I'm sorry, but the boys have just torn out the rotten window in the master bedroom, so unless you want to sleep in a freezing cold bed covered in brick dust, there's not much I can do. I've really got to get back, but I'll keep you updated."

He disappeared through the front door, leaving Genny in the front garden with a bewildered look on her face. She peered through after him, wondering if it was as unfinished as he had told her. It seemed the red wooden door - adorned with the original foxglove-shaped brass knocker - was just about the only thing stood upright. The kitchen was coated in plastic, either ready to be removed or ready to be put in, she couldn't quite tell. There were bundles of wires hanging down from each room's ceilings, and from her vantage point in the hallway she could just about make out the living room, which was missing half of its floorboards.

With a defeated sigh, she locked the moving truck and leaned against the driver's side door, looking up at the mess that was her little cottage.

She had known it was a fixer upper when she'd bought it in an online auction, cheap as chips, understandably – a little detached Victorian red brick, part and parcel with the old bakery next door, which had been vacant for years after the previous owners had passed away.

She had researched the location meticulously – Whitebourne village, a sleepy community set along the eponymous River Whitebourne, with protected historic buildings and within a short walk of some of the best beaches Solent Island had to offer. Solent Island was already a home from home for her, having spent so many summers here in her childhood with her parents and sister, Annabelle.

She had done everything right. She had emailed the council to check the bylaws. She had contacted a contractor with good reviews on HonestyCompass and set a realistic schedule for the work.

The 5th – that had been the plan. Or so she had thought.

Her new life wasn't quite off to the start she had envisioned.

Mitchell appeared at the door again and noticed that she was still outside. He sighed to himself and zipped up his red and green tartan fleece as he headed out into the cold street to talk to her.

"Don't despair," he shrugged, trying to offer some awkward but well-intentioned comfort. "We're still under budget and working just as fast as we can. In the meantime, there's a bed and breakfast in town – *The Mudlark Inn*. The owners, Tom and Bev, are in their late 70s now and slowing down a bit, so they don't take in as many tourists these days, but they do a good full English. If you tell them about your situation, I'm sure they can give you a good discount."

"I don't suppose they're dog friendly?" Genny asked, pointing to Pip, her speckled brown and white Springer Spaniel, who was sat in the van with her nose pushed as far out of the cracked window as she could, desperate to see the island.

"You'll find it's quite a dog friendly island all round. I've got a chocolate lab myself," Mitchell nodded. "I'm sure you'll find no resistance to a sweet-looking dog like that."

He offered Pip his hand to sniff and cooed affectionately at the dog as she responded with frantic tail wagging.

"Thank you, Mitchell," Genny smiled, although inside she was still trying to reconcile how the day had gone so quickly out of hand. "I really appreciate your help."

"Try to guess how our inn got its name," Bev Beecham chattered excitedly as she led Genny to her room, Pip padding up ahead of them with an anticipatory whine.

They had insisted on giving her the room for free until the 15th when she had told them about her issues with the cottage, despite her protests. They were already some of the most decent people Genny had ever met, and although they snipped back and forth as Bev's husband Tom carried the luggage up the stairs – again at his insistence – they were clearly very much in love.

"Mudlark?" Genny said, trying to recall hearing the word before.

The inn was by the north bank of the River Whitebourne, the largest river on Solent Island both by volume, width and length, and it seemed the village was very much centred around it, with several old bridges snaking over it and shopfronts making the most of their proximity to it.

"That's right, *mudlark*," Tom answered with a twinkling emphasis on the word, as if it was a clue all in itself.

"Well, my first instinct is to say that it is named after a bird, perhaps a wader on the riverbank," Genny said after a moment. "But…"

"Oh! She has a 'but', Tom!" Bev said excitedly. "Very few people come up with a 'but'."

"But…" Genny continued. "I remember the term from a book I read about Victorian London some years ago, during my degree. I think a mudlark was a scavenger of sorts, someone who collected scrap and potentially treasure from the banks of the river."

"She's got it, Bev!" Tom chuckled, slightly out of breath from the stairs as they reached the corridor and headed towards the room.

"She certainly has, Tom!" Bev giggled. "Oh, aren't you a bright lady? Let me guess – you're a lawyer up there in The Big Smoke?"

"No, no," Genny said. "I'm in between careers at the moment while the bakery is fixed up."

"But you did have a job in London?" Tom asked. "We love London when we go to the mainland, don't we Bev?"

"We do! Tom - don't crowd her!" Bev nagged, as Tom shrugged apologetically. "So, not a lawyer. Something else very intelligent – a university professor?"

Genny tried to hide her tension with a half-smile as she replied, "I was a Detective Inspector with the police force before I retired."

"Oh! A detective, do you hear that, Tom?"

"I certainly do, my love," Tom replied, unlocking the door to Genny's room. "A real clever pants."

The room was spacious, kitted out with all the basics, although it was less modern than she had hoped. The en suite was avocado green with an overhead flush on the toilet and only a cold tap on the sink.

But no matter the tiny things she could nit-pick, today they were her knights in shining armour.

"It is just perfect," Genny smiled, looking out of the view from the window over the river and across Whitebourne. "Are you sure that you won't accept any money from me? I really feel terrible taking away a room from paying customers."

"Oh, don't be silly, love," Bev said with a dismissive wave of her hand. "October is not a busy time of year on the island even for the tourist trap inns, and we're just a tiny place. We only have one other guest at the moment, a quiet gentlemen, he doesn't even come down for breakfast. The rest of the rooms were just sat here empty!"

"Well, if you're sure," Genny smiled. "I'm very grateful."

"Don't mention it," Tom beamed. "You just get settled in and you let us know if you need anything."

They turned to leave, Bev stopping short of the doorway and adding, "We're all going to the lighthouse re-opening this evening, if you'd like to come along? Most of the island will be there, so it would be a good chance for you to get to know your neighbours and potential future customers."

"The lighthouse re-opening?" Genny asked.

"Haven't you heard about it?" Bev replied. "It's the talk of the island!"

"No, I haven't," Genny admitted. "I just got off of a ferry in Solan thirty minutes ago."

"Oh, well," Tom grinned. "It's quite a big news story around here. Sandhaven Lighthouse – over the river, halfway between here and Westmarsh - has been out of commission for… oh, decades! A developer from London bought it and is re-opening it this evening."

Normally, Genny would have preferred to stay home and read a book or take Pip out for a walk, but it did sound like an easy opportunity to get to know her new neighbours and explore parts of the island she hadn't been to since she was a child.

She vaguely remembered Sandhaven Lighthouse – still in working order during her childhood – surrounded by the protected Nature Reserve and wetlands around the river. She and Annabelle had preferred the beaches along the estuary, but she had a clear memory of the lighthouse up above them on the clifftop, a constant, calming presence; a promise of protection for those down below.

"It sounds great," Genny said.

Bev and Tom shared an excited glance before Bev added, "You can't be older than forty – are you married? Children?"

Genny blinked, a little taken aback by the direct questions. She was starting to get the feeling Bev and Tom wouldn't be the only overbearingly friendly people on this island.

"Forty-four," she corrected. "And no to both."

"Oh, well, there's still time!" Bev said sheepishly, realising she had put her foot in her mouth. Tom nudged her and whispered something in her ear, Genny watching them with puzzled bemusement. "Forty-four…" Bev added. "I'm sure we know some fine chaps around that age."

"That's… that's great," Genny replied, not sure how to tell these sweet people not to set her up with random men, regardless of whether or not they were her age.

"Well, we'll leave you to freshen up," Tom said. "We'll be leaving to go to the lighthouse at 5pm. It's just a short walk over the Queen Victoria Bridge and then through the wetlands."

And with that, they left her and Pip, whittering enthusiastically to each other about the men they would set her up with.

Genny unpacked her suitcase and set to making herself a cup of tea with the amenities left for her on the side. A kettle sat next to a traditional teapot, covered with a teal tea cosy. There was a selection of tea bags, coffee sachets, and UHT milk, the packaging for which proudly declared that it was from a dairy just outside of Whitebourne.

"Everything is local here, Pip," Genny beamed.

She boiled the kettle and chose a teabag, brewing a full pot.

She paused as she placed the teal tea cosy back on top. Something about it reminded her of Annabelle, and a memory came, unbidden, as they often did.

"Will you please stop worrying about me? It's only a half an hour walk," Annabelle had laughed, her voice slightly wobbly from the half a bottle of wine

they had shared over dinner, pulling down her teal dress as it slid above her knees.

"It's freezing! Won't you let DS Hutton take you home?" Genny had said, getting ready to text her partner to bring the car around, a cheeky use of police resources but for her baby sister she was happy to bend the rules.

"Why won't you just call him Rob? He's been your police partner for over a year now, you can loosen up and be friends with the man, you know," Annabelle had chided.

"Anna, he's my colleague," Genny said firmly. "If you won't let him drive you, I'll walk with you. London can be unsafe at night."

"And let you walk back alone? It's the same amount of danger either way."

"I can handle myself," Genny had insisted.

"So can I," Annabelle had smirked, stepping out into the road with a wave.

Genny shuddered and moved back from the teapot, Pip springing up onto the bed to lick her face and hands.

"I'm fine, I'm fine," Genny whispered to Pip. "I'm fine…"

She tried to remember the grounding techniques the police therapist had taught her.

Count the objects in the room. Count the number of colours you could see. Count your body parts, head to toes.

The first one worked this time. 43 objects in the room, 12 of those were sugar packets in a vintage can which had once contained nuts.

She let her breath flow out of her.

Her phone started to vibrate where it lay on the bedsheets, flashing up the name 'Mum'.

She took a final, longer breath and answered.

"How's the new house?!" Her mum asked without waiting for Genny to say anything first, her excitement coming out in her squealing high-pitched tone. "Oh, I can just picture it in my head now. I can't wait to visit!"

"There was a bit of a snafu actually," Genny said, laying back on the bed with Pip nestling into her arm, her heart still beating faster than normal. "The cottage and bakery aren't ready. I'm currently at an inn in the village."

"What? But you spoke to the builder! Is he one of those dodgy scammers? There was a programme on the television about them last night – one lady had all of her copper pipes stolen!" Her mum replied.

"No, Mum," Genny laughed. "We got our dates mixed up. He seems like a nice enough guy."

"They always do," her mum insisted. "Then they steal all of your nubbins."

"What's a nubbin?"

"I don't know, I'm not a builder," her mum answered, and Genny tried to hide a snort of laughter.

"Don't worry about me, Mum."

"You sound tired – are you tired?"

"A little," Genny agreed.

There was a pause and then her mum asked quietly, "Were you thinking about Annabelle?"

The question hung between them as Genny stayed silent for a moment, finally croaking out, "Yes."

"Oh, sweetheart," her mum replied. "I understand. She loved the island – all those summers you both spent on the beach. It's bound to remind you of her. But it's been two years since the accident… she would want you to have a fresh start."

Genny nodded, trying to hold back the sobs which threatened to overcome her.

In truth, London had reminded her of Annabelle more and more.

The hospital she had spent her final hours.

The corner of Yew Street and Kirk Avenue where the hit and run had happened.

The police station where Genny and DS Hutton had worked tirelessly to try to find the killer.

These were all places she knew she could never return to, places which symbolised the worst period of her entire life.

Solent Island brought her happy memories of Annabelle – which was in part why she had chosen it for her new life - but that didn't stop the occasional flash of regret, a memory played over and over, words analysed for any hint of who had killed her baby sister.

"I know, Mum," Genny managed eventually.

Her mum was still quiet on the other end of the line. Besides her dad, she was the only other person who knew what she had been through, the only other person who shared every inch of her grief.

"So, tell me about this inn you're staying in – is it nice?"

"It's... very sweet of them to put me up," Genny said, looking around the room. "The owners are keen to go to the re-opening of some lighthouse this evening. I might go along."

"You should! It would be good to mix with the locals."

"I think so too. The owners are about your age, they've been here all their lives from what they told me."

"I wonder if we ever stayed there when you were children. Dad might remember – I'll ask him when he gets in from the allotment."

"Still up there every day?"

"Every single day. It's broccoli season at the moment, apparently. It's all he talks about."

Losing Annabelle had been hard on all of them, but no one more than their Dad.

"Parents aren't meant to bury their children," he'd wept as Genny gripped his arm tightly at the gravesite.

Genny swallowed down the echo of his words and painted a smile on her face, replying, "I look forward to a roast dinner with his famous broccoli when I come to visit."

"Settle in first, love. Don't feel you need to rush back to London for us."

"Today, I am able to make history," a wide-set man with short black hair and a tailored suit projected out to the crowd, gathered around the rear of the lighthouse, the roaring sea a few hundred metres below them. Bev and Tom had explained to Genny on the walk that this was Kristian Nobel, the developer from London. They had gushed about him and his plan to save the lighthouse, but from the looks on the faces of the crowd members, not everyone felt the same. Some were bored, some were confused, and others were angry.

"As you may know, this lighthouse was once manned, but since the last lighthouse keeper left the post two decades ago, it has sat here, made derelict by the passing of time, even the iconic red stripe fading and peeling away. The story of the building's past moved me, and I knew I had to be part of its future," he continued.

"Isn't he great?" Bev murmured to Genny, who raised an eyebrow in reply.

"Just a year ago, after a long battle with the Solent Island Wetland Society, I was able to purchase this land and set my plan for a new, more modern Sandhaven in motion," Kristian said.

Genny took him in. He was fifty or so, and the polar opposite of the crowd dressed in walking gear and cosy jumpers. She couldn't help but wonder how his sparkling leather shoes and tailored suit had remained so clean given the walk up to the lighthouse.

By his side was a young woman, no older than her mid-twenties, with the same dark hair as him, cut in a sharp line just above her shoulders. She too was dressed for a different location, with thin high heels which were sinking into the grass every time she shifted her weight, and a grey dress, ideal for office-attire but jarring in the current circumstance.

"Today, the new, improved lighthouse is ready," Kristian said, his voice unnecessarily thunderous.

Genny looked around as someone scoffed. She couldn't make out who, but she saw disgust mirrored in a few of the faces around her.

Reporters clicked their cameras as Kristian posed with some ceremonial scissors, comically large, and cut through a ribbon which had been draped around the lighthouse.

Genny noticed a man with black hair and stubble near the front, arms crossed with the patient expression of someone who attended a lot of these events. He was wearing black trousers, a shirt and tie, but if at one point in the day he had been wearing a suit jacket, it was replaced now by a dark green waterproof coat, and instead of loafers, he wore walking boots.

"That's Detective Inspector Remy Cochran," Bev whispered to Genny, noticing her eyeline. "He's on our list to set you up with."

"Oh really?" Genny whispered back with an amused grin.

"He's a little younger than you – mid-30s maybe, but he's a real catch," Bev continued.

"A bit of a loner, though," Tom interjected.

"Don't tell her that," Bev muttered, tapping him playfully on the arm in rebuke. "She'll think he's odd."

Of course, he was a detective – that explained the attire and the patient if slightly vacant look on his face. She had been in that mode many times herself, watching a parade or community art project, vigilant and silent even in her downtime.

"Welcome to the new Sandhaven Lighthouse!" Kristian said as he put down the scissors to a smattering of applause.

Genny felt Pip shift from her sitting position at Genny's feet as someone near the back right-hand side of the group broke away quietly – a man with greying dark hair and a red jacket, sixty or a little older. She couldn't quite see his face in the fading sunlight, but his body language was defensive, hunched and moving quickly back down the cliffside towards Whitebourne. No one else seemed to notice him leave.

"If you would all like to head around to the entrance with me, we can go inside and enjoy some champagne," the young woman said, an unnaturally crescent-shaped smile stretching across her face as she did.

"That's Mr. Nobel's daughter," Tom explained. "Roisin."

The crowd seemed to pep up at the mention of free alcohol and Genny followed the Beechams as they moved towards the front door on the opposite side of the lighthouse.

A scream went up somewhere near the front of the group, and as more people reached the far side of the lighthouse, the sound repeated throughout them, a chain reaction of fear and horror. The crowd seemed to stop in its tracks as the people at the front spoke in low tones, and the people behind tried to crane to see.

Genny knew that sound all too well.

She and Pip pushed forward, rushing to the front.

There, strewn on the steps of the new lighthouse, was the body of Mitchell Collins, eyes open wide and a gunshot wound to the chest, covered from head to toe in red liquid.

2

"Everyone stand back, stand back!" DI Cochran forced his way to the body, holding up his police badge. He placed his fingers on the side of Mitchell's neck, although Genny could tell from the wounds and empty eyes that the poor man was already gone. Remy was resigned to the same conclusion. He hesitated with a morose look before returning to his pragmatic tone. "This is a police matter, please get back!"

"Is he dead?!" Someone shouted from the group.

"Yes, sadly," DI Cochran said, pulling his mobile phone from his pocket and ringing someone. The crowd fell into hysterics, some shepherding others away, and some struggling to stay standing in shock. Genny kept her attention on the DI. "Sandra, there's been a murder up at Sandhaven Lighthouse – a man in his mid-60s, Mitchell Collins. Send for an ambulance and bring a team up here right away. Okay. Okay, alright. Thank you."

As he hung up the phone Bev caught up to Genny, grabbing her arm, "Isn't it terrible?"

"Awful," Genny agreed, putting a comforting arm around Bev's shoulder and ushering her towards a nearby bench. "Come and sit down. The ambulance and police will be here soon."

Paramedics were the first on the scene, confirming DI Cochran's assertion; Mitchell Collins was dead. A police team arrived within minutes, the sirens whistling up the cliff. They left their cars on the other side of the protected Nature Reserve and traipsed up to the lighthouse on foot.

Genny sat with Bev, comforting her and Tom as best she could.

In truth, she was more shaken by the events than she might have usually been. Years of detective work had prepared her for most situations, but she felt an odd affinity to the man who only a few hours earlier had been working on her new home.

But she wasn't a detective anymore, and the police would take care of it. She tried to remind herself of that fact as the team taped off the scene, and DI

Cochran started to move amongst the group, taking witness statements.

It was hard not to have all of her attention on him, calculating whether she would have done the same as him, had she been the detective on this case.

Would she put her hand on the shoulder of the crying Roisin Nobel? Would she try to get a list of attendees? Would she try to stop people from leaving?

Despite her critical eye on him, she saw that he and his team were indeed diligent, methodically setting up the crime scene as the forensic photographer got to work. They moved everyone away from the body, and a pair of PCs set up a tent over the crime scene, shielding the distressing sight from the crowd. Poles connected by police tape were set up to cordon the area off.

"You were a detective in London, weren't you?" Bev asked Genny tearfully.

"Yes," Genny said, remembering their earlier conversation.

"Do you think this was a murder?" Bev asked, bottom lip wobbling at the thought.

Genny pictured the scene as they'd found it.

The wound on Mitchell's chest had certainly been consistent with gunshot wounds Genny had seen before. A small island community like this, mostly made up of farmers, retired folk, tourists and rich people's second homes, were unlikely candidates for a gun crime, but it wasn't unheard of. If anyone on the island had a gun, it would be more likely to be a shotgun – a farmer's fox scarer and nothing more.

The fact that it was a small, single wound meant it was more likely to be a handgun, up close.

Deliberate.

"Let's just wait and see what the police say," Genny said with a gentle squeeze of Bev's hand. "They'll tell us all they can."

The Nobels were stood nearby, Kristian with his head down as he replied to emails on his phone, and Roisin crying softly next to him.

DI Cochran reached the Nobels, and Genny was finally able to overhear the conversation, tuning out Tom and Bev soothing one another next to her.

"Mr. Nobel, Miss Nobel, I just have a few questions," the DI said, pen poised over a notepad.

"Is this a formal interview?" Kristian shot back, reluctantly putting his phone back into his pocket. "If so, I will ring my lawyer."

"No," the DI said. "My team and I are just trying to establish what happened here. Your co-operation would really be appreciated in this matter."

"Fine," Kristian said tersely. "Ask away."

"Thank you," the DI said. Genny marvelled at this restraint. The way he kept his face completely blank as he ran through his questions was masterful. "Had you met Mr. Collins, the victim, before today?"

"Yes," Kristian shrugged, pushing his hands into the pockets of his suit trousers. "I hired his company to complete the work on the lighthouse."

"And were you satisfied with his work?"

"Of course! What are you implying – that I didn't think his paintwork was good enough, so I shot him and left his body on the steps of the lighthouse to be discovered by the entire island?"

"I'm not implying anything, Mr. Nobel," DI Cochran replied simply, still calm and collected. "I'm just trying to establish what happened to our victim. How would you describe Mr. Collins? Was he professional, cordial, timely?"

"Again, I really resent the implication that I would kill someone because they weren't on time to a job," Kristian bristled.

"He was always very friendly," Roisin piped up.

"Thank you, Miss Nobel," DI Cochran said, still unphased by Kristian's indignation. "Did you ever see him taking long phone calls or arguing with anyone? His employees, perhaps?"

"No," Roisin shrugged, dabbing her nose with a tissue as she thought about her answer. "Long phone calls, sometimes. But he was never secretive about them. They seemed like work calls to me. He would argue with his son, Jake, about the work mostly. You know how parents and their kids can get."

Kristian gave her a sidewards look.

"I see," DI Cochran nodded. "And Jake worked with Mr. Collins on the lighthouse?"

"I think he worked with him on all of his projects," Roisin agreed. "They were often the only two up here, staying after hours to get it finished on time."

"Thank you for your co-operation," DI Cochran said with a brief half-smile. "I'll be in touch if we need any more information from you."

Roisin nodded, but Kristian took offense at the final phrase, adding in a furious whisper, "You know, it's not us who you should be pointing fingers at! It's those bloody protestors from the SIWS! That little psycho Skye and her pals threw paint all over the lighthouse when construction began! They'd do anything to make tonight a disaster!"

"Thank you for your concern, Mr. Nobel," the DI said, taking a deep breath. "We will be conducting a thorough investigation and considering all possible suspects."

With that, he moved on, leaving Kristian seething.

He approached Genny and the Beechams with a small smile.

"Hello, Bev, Tom, sorry that you are wrapped up in all of this," he said, catching Genny off guard with how familiar he was being compared to his previously professional tone. "I just have a few questions. And I don't believe we've met?"

He turned his attention to Genny.

"She was a detective too," Bev interjected before Genny could answer. "In London!"

"Is that right?" DI Cochran smiled softly.

"Genny Hadley. Yes, I *was* a DI in London, but I have taken a new career path now," Genny answered.

"As what?" The DI asked, taking notes.

"Mitchell Collins was actually renovating Foxglove Cottage in Whitebourne for me. I am going to re-open the old bakery there."

"A very different career path, if you don't mind me saying," DI Cochran commented. "So, how many times had you met Mitchell Collins?"

"Just today – I arrived at the cottage to find we had miscommunicated via email, and it wouldn't be ready for another couple of weeks," Genny explained. "That was the first time we had met face to face."

"I see," DI Cochran nodded. "And what time was this?"

She would have asked the same. Establishing a timeline – if they knew what time Mitchell was last seen, they could narrow down alibis while they waited for the official time of death to be determined.

"Around 3.20pm," Genny said. "Bev and Tom should be able to corroborate that as I arrived at *The Mudlark* ten or so minutes after that.

"That's right," Bev sniffled. "We checked her in at pretty much 3.30pm on the dot."

"Very precise, thank you," DI Cochran smiled. "I know this may not seem relevant, but all the information I can gather now could help me work out what happened to Mr. Collins – were you upset when you found out that you had miscommunicated about the timeframe of your renovation? You had to find somewhere else to stay, by the sounds of it. I presume you travelled all the way from London by plane or ferry, and you've had to find somewhere to store your possessions?"

She would also have asked that.

She was the newcomer, an outsider, an unknown. He had to imply that she had a motive, and her reaction would tell just as much as the motive itself.

Genny kept her tone the same, and was honest with him, "That's all true – I had a long journey and had to find accommodation. My possessions are still locked in the moving truck I hired for the day, and I expect I will have to pay to hire it for another week or more. It has all been very inconvenient to me, and not the way I wanted to start my new life on the island. That said, it was not Mr. Collins' fault. It was a miscommunication. These things happen."

"I understand," DI Cochran nodded, scribbling down yet more notes. "I appreciate your candour. Did any of you see anything suspicious during the event? Anyone that you didn't recognise here?"

Genny thought of the man that had walked off, but although she had never seen him before, she didn't know anyone else on Solent Island either. She had no way of knowing if that was unusual. She decided it wasn't worth mentioning, unless someone else had thought he was suspicious too. She looked to Bev and Tom.

"No," Tom shrugged. "It was just the usual suspects here – sorry, bad wording – just the usual folk."

Bev nudged him scoldingly for the 'suspects' comment.

"Okay, thank you," DI Cochran nodded. "I'll be in touch if we need any more information from you. How can I reach you?" He added to Genny.

"At the inn," Genny said. "Or I can provide my phone number?"

"I think that would be best," DI Cochran said.

"You can't possibly think Genny was involved, Remy?!" Bev sputtered.

"Bev, let the man do his job," Tom reassured her.

"You have my full co-operation, DI Cochran," Genny said, digging into her handbag and ripping the side off of a cardboard sandwich box she had bought at Solan ferry station and started writing her number onto it.

"Call me Remy, please," he said with an uncharacteristically warm smile, before moving on to the next group of people.

"Remy," Genny nodded, returning his smile.

Genny couldn't sleep that night, images of Mitchell and the gloomy lighthouse swimming in her mind.

Despite her best efforts to push the case from her mind, in between fits of sleep, she was trying to piece together motives, suspects, and an explanation for who would want to kill him.

The dreams morphed – she was on the beach below the lighthouse, looking up as Annabelle stepped out across the sand, her hand just lifting into a wave as a car sped towards her.

Genny woke up in a cold sweat, Pip jumping up onto the bed and licking her face with an empathetic whine.

"I'm okay, Pip," Genny whispered to her, trying to calm her hammering heart.

The sun was coming up, the inn's faded old curtains doing little to block out the light.

She headed down to breakfast, finding Bev and Tom setting out two tables – one for her and one for the male guest they had mentioned yesterday.

"He hasn't come down so far during his stay," Bev explained. "But we set the table just in case."

"How long has he been staying here?" Genny asked. "Has he not left the room at all?"

"Three days. And I think he has," Tom said in a hushed tone. "Sometimes I hear the front door close, and I think to myself that it must be him coming or going. Some guests are like that. Not social."

Genny nodded and sat down at the table. She ordered a full English with poached eggs, hoping the sustenance would revive her after a restless night.

"You know," Bev said, as she poured Genny some tea. "There is a dog walkers' group at the pub in town today – *The Water's Edge*. If you're looking to make some friends and see more of the local area, you might enjoy it. Take your mind off everything that happened yesterday."

"Thank you, I think I will do just that," Genny said. She added with a chuckle, "I had expected to be baking cakes this week to get everything ready to open my bakery. How quickly things change."

"And I suppose the renovation work will be halted now that… well, now…" Bev said, a catch in her throat as she was reminded of Mitchell again.

"I suppose so," Genny nodded sadly. She hadn't even considered it. The tragedy of Mitchell's death was going to have a huge ripple effect across the community.

"Well, you can stay here as long as you need to – *gratis*, of course," Bev assured her.

"You are far too kind and generous," Genny smiled. "I don't know if I can expect you to let me stay here for free indefinitely. Let me at least pay a discounted rate."

"Nonsense," Bev waved her hand as if swatting an annoying fly. "It is the Solent Island way. We look after people here. You just focus on getting settled into the community."

And so, after breakfast, Genny packed a rucksack, and pulled on walking boots before she and Pip headed out to *The Water's Edge*.

It was a quiet, traditional English pub. A plaque on the front wall told Genny that it was originally built in 1862, in anticipation of the arrival of Queen Victoria, who was due to summer at her Solent Island home, Yaxley Manor.

The design was mock Tudor, with low wooden beams on the inside, and yet still obviously Victorian with red bricks and wrought iron everywhere.

The dog walkers' group was gathered outside, chatting and trying to stop their overexcited dogs from playing with each other as they waited to get started. She wasn't initially sure who was in charge until a couple of people moved and a woman Genny's age with a clipboard became obvious. She was wearing a bright pink bodywarmer and her blonde bob was pushed back by a turquoise headband.

"Hi, I'm here for the dog walkers' group," Genny said as she approached her.

"Ah!" The woman beamed with delight. "You must be Genny Hadley – everyone's been talking about you!"

"Oh?" Genny asked, turning to look over her shoulder with concern as other members of the group seemed to notice her and quieten.

"Yes, we heard all about your mix-up with the renovation, how embarrassing!" The woman laughed and seeing the stony look on Genny's face quickly added. "These things happen."

"Yes, they do."

"And so tragic about Mitchell Collins of course."

"It is awful," Genny agreed.

"Well, the police will catch the killer," the woman said with a firm nod. "Anyway, I'm Polly Montford-Blake, and these are the other Whitebourne dog walkers – Tenisha, Gertie and Niamh."

The other women raised their hands in greeting. They were a little more 'Stepford wives' than Genny's usual crowd in London, falling straight into conversations about their husbands as Genny stood listening, but they seemed harmless enough. They were wealthy – she could see that it in the sparkling diamond rings and overpriced sportswear, but they seemed less interested in talking about their wealth than about their social lives, or their families.

She knew communities like this all too well – airbrushed and aesthetic from the outside, but hotbeds for gossip and crime in private. She had found that with entitlement, the wealthy also had a surprising righteousness when it came to breaking the law.

"I'm making Greg a stew tonight," Polly explained. "Beef, although I am always trying to get him to eat something leaner."

"We're on a pinto bean kick at the moment," Tenisha countered as she tied her hair back. "Jeff just loves them."

"Are you married, Genny?" Polly asked suddenly, catching her off-guard.

"No," she said, a little too quickly for their liking. "I just never found the right person," she clarified as they looked at her with horror.

"Well, I'm sure it isn't too late," Polly replied cattily, leaning down to unclip her dog's leash and turning to the whole group. "Everyone! We're going to take the blue route along the clifftop today to avoid the crime scene – poor Mitchell, may he rest in peace – and then loop back up from Westmarsh over the river. The walk will take about an hour, longer if you decide to stop at *The Dog and Bull* in Westmarsh for a drink."

"I'm going to need a glass of white if we're taking the blue route," Tenisha whispered to Genny, as if they were now confidantes. "The steep hills are a thigh killer."

Genny nodded conspiratorially, wondering why on earth these women signed up to the dog walking group if the idea of the walk itself made them reach for alcohol.

The blue route up the cliffs was certainly steeper than the route they had taken to the lighthouse the day before, but Genny and Pip revelled in the rolling views out across the sea, trying to hang back from the little group of women they had become attached to; Genny had nothing to add to conversations about what sort of toilet bleach was best.

After half an hour or so, they came to *The Dog and Bull*, and Polly insisted on buying everyone a drink.

"Shall I just get a bottle of Pinot Grigio for everyone?" She asked, looking around at the group who nodded enthusiastically. Her gaze stopped on Genny, noticing she hadn't joined in. "Is wine okay for you? I can get you a G&T if you prefer?"

"Oh, I actually don't drink," Genny said.

The group looked at her as if she had said she killed puppies.

"Never?" Niamh asked with a disgusted downward turn of her mouth. "Not even… on Christmas?"

"No," Genny shrugged.

Polly leaned in and murmured, "Are you an alcoholic? It's okay if you are. I think Tenisha might be one too."

"Hey!" Tenisha protested. "Don't joke about that kind of thing. Alcoholism ruins lives. You don't have to tell us, Genny."

"It's fine," Genny replied with an awkward chuckle. "I'm not an alcoholic, I just don't drink anymore. I'll get myself a soft drink, don't worry."

She wasn't sure whether it was the lack of alcohol or the insisting for paying for her own drink that Polly took offense to, but she wrinkled up her nose as Genny asked the bar maid for an apple juice.

The group found a table by the fireplace and the gossip started to flow.

"It's so sad about Mitchell," Niamh said.

"So sad that he died like that," Polly agreed. "He was a real DILF."

"A DILF? Who even says that anymore," Tenisha bristled. "And let's not talk about a dead man like that. It's not respectful."

Genny was starting to get the impression that Polly said whatever she liked, and despite the protests from the others, they still hung on her every word.

"Why not?" Polly said boldly. "He wasn't exactly a nice chap, let's not change our tune just because of how tragic his death was."

"How so?" Genny asked, intrigued. She hadn't heard anyone say a word against Mitchell, and even if Polly seemed to be a pretty unreliable source, she couldn't help but want to hear.

"He was well-known in the community for overpricing building jobs," Polly shrugged. "When he did our kitchen, he added another thousand onto the price at the end for 'extra labour'. You can't just go around doing that and getting away with it."

"Really?" Genny asked. "He was doing the work on my place, and he never asked for extra money."

"I don't suppose he got the chance," Tenisha said, reluctantly adding. "Polly's right, he did that a lot. He also had a lot of animosity with his son, Jake, who worked for him. It meant that sometimes the projects dragged on and on because they would refuse to speak to each other."

"Why didn't they get on?" Genny asked.

"I don't know," Tenisha said. "Normal father and son stuff, I'm sure."

Genny tried to imagine what 'normal father and son stuff' would result in them not speaking for so long that building projects would end up delayed, but she didn't push the idea.

The pub door opened, letting in a waft of cold air as Kristian and Roisin Nobel walked in. Kristian was on his phone, dressed in a different suit, looking just as put together as he had at the lighthouse, whilst Roisin looked drawn and tired, wearing a crinkled skirt suit.

"Oh, now, talking of DILFs…" Polly said as he walked in. "That man could have me anytime."

The others giggled at the thought. Genny kept her face as blank as she could.

"He doesn't seem to fit in with the rest of the islanders," Genny suggested. "Does he live here full-time? Bev and Tom from *The Mudlark* told me he was originally from London."

"Half and half," Tenisha explained. "It was a huge scandal when he first bought his house here – the big one by Grove Bend bridge in Whitebourne. The locals weren't very pleased to have a businessman flashing his cash in town."

"They are all just jealous," Polly asserted. "He's not as wealthy as Greg."

Genny resisted the desire to laugh as Polly mentioned her husband for the tenth time in half an hour. She sipped her apple juice to hide her smirk.

"He started buying everything, that's why everyone hates him," Gertie murmured, the first time she had spoken since the walk and already two glasses of wine in. "First, he bought the Victorian biscuit factory in Westmarsh and turned it into some trendy restaurant where everything comes on a mouldy plank of wood. Then he bought a parcel of land between Gentleweir and Whitebourne and tried to get planning permission for 200 houses. The Solent Island Preservation Society stopped him."

"Sounds like he's had a lot of trouble with the island's societies," Genny remarked. "He mentioned in his speech at the lighthouse re-opening that the Solent Island Wetland Society tried to stop him renovating it."

"They did," Niamh nodded. "Their supporters protested. It nearly ended the whole project."

"I hear something about a 'Skye' somebody?" Genny offered, remembering the name from DI Cochran's questions to Kristian the day before.

"Skye Devon – the leader of the little protest club," Polly said. "If it wasn't bad enough that we have some self-aggrandising tycoon building on our island, we had to endure all manner of ridiculous stunts put on by the protestors."

"You didn't approve of their protests?"

"Of course not!" Polly laughed. "Skye Devon and her silly followers are the worst sort of people. They want to rock the boat no matter what, and they will find a way to do it, even if it isn't legal."

Genny noticed Kristian at the bar and saw an opportunity.

"I'm just going to get some ice for my apple juice," Genny said, excusing herself from the table.

She headed to the bar, positioning herself along from Kristian just as he was hanging up the phone.

"Please, no more work calls," Roisin begged him.

"Stop it, Ro," Kristian said. "Daddy has to work."

Genny grimaced – Roisin was clearly in her mid-twenties, the infantilisation was cringe-inducing.

"You promised that once the lighthouse was open that we'd do something fun," Ro whined.

"Well, the lighthouse isn't exactly open," Kristian bit back at her. "Now that some dumb builder's gone and gotten himself killed in front of it. God knows how long it will take to get the mess cleaned up – both literally and the mess my reputation is in. Who is going to want to visit a lighthouse that was the scene of a murder?"

"We'll hire a top marketing advisor," Ro said brightly. "Someone who can get everyone to forget. Tourists won't know a thing about the murder."

Genny asked the barmaid for ice for her apple juice, drawing the Nobels' attention to her.

"You were at the opening yesterday," Kristian said with a smarmy smile. "I'd know that beautiful face and stunning red hair anywhere. Are you a reporter?"

"No," Genny said, ignoring the obvious charm offensive. "Just a resident of Whitebourne."

"Oh, we might be neighbours," Kristian grinned. "I'll be sure to come over for a cup of sugar."

"No, thank you," Genny said, adding quietly to only him, as she turned and headed back to her table. "Not if you were the last man on the island."

His face fell as he watched her walk away, turning back to his phone.

3

Genny managed to ditch the dog walking group by dinner time, no doubt all returning home to cook stews for their husbands and fantasise about Kristian Nobel.

She chose a small table back in Whitebourne in *The Water's Edge* and ordered dinner, glad to be only be in her own company at last.

She had always been comfortable by herself, just observing people and enjoying the quiet, something she had hoped to have more of with the move to Solent Island.

The pub was bustling with people, a few that she recognised from the lighthouse re-opening, and a few stragglers from the Sunday dog walking group.

She was surprised to also see Kristian Nobel, without Roisin this time, sat at a table with a young woman with bright blue hair and tattoos up her arms. They were talking in hushed tones, but Kristian's face was contorted in rage as he listened to her. Genny tried to make out what they were saying, but the woman kept obscuring her mouth with her hand.

After a few minutes, Kristian hissed something with unbridled rage, before leaving the pub. The woman stared at the table for a moment, composing herself, and then left too.

"Here we are – the butternut squash and pecan salad," the barmaid, Imogen, said as she brought over Genny's dinner. "And a bowl of water for the beautiful pupper."

Pip wagged her tail excitedly, lapping up the fresh water after their long walk around the cliffs.

"Thank you," Genny smiled. "Can I ask – who was the woman with blue hair who was in here just a minute ago?"

"Oh, you mean Skye? Skye Devon?" Imogen said. "She's a regular in here, although she keeps herself to herself."

"Skye Devon," Genny repeated.

That was the name of the protestor Polly had mentioned, and Genny had heard Kristian mention to DI Cochran. Why was Kristian arguing with her if the lighthouse was already open? Did he suspect her of murdering Mitchell Collins? He had said just that to DI Cochran, but Genny had presumed he was exaggerating.

"She's not terribly popular in Whitebourne anymore," Imogen said, lowering her voice and looking around. "Her protest group TP-ed the town in the summer."

"What is TP-ing?" Genny asked, perplexed.

"Toilet paper – they buy packs and packs of it and write protest slogans on it before throwing it all over people's houses, cars, streetlamps, anything they can. We've only just gotten it all cleaned up. People were finding little bits of white paper on everything they owned for months."

"That doesn't seem to go along with the whole environmentalism thing," Genny pointed out.

"They claimed that making the statement was more important than the temporary impact," Imogen said, using mocking air quotes. "I'm not sure they made the statement they were hoping to. Their protests have angered more people than they have mobilised. Lots of us care about the wetlands, about conservation and the environment, but we go about showing it in different ways. Petitions, fundraisers, local clean-up missions. All Skye and her ilk are doing are alienating the community."

"It certainly seems that way," Genny sighed.

"Sorry for talking your ear off," Imogen shrugged. "Enjoy your food."

"Thanks, and there's nothing to apologise for. You've been really helpful."

So perhaps it wasn't only Kristian that was growing impatient with Skye Devon. But did she actually have anything to do with Mitchell Collins' murder? It was quite a leap to go from throwing toilet paper onto houses to shooting someone in cold blood.

The pub door opened again, and DI Cochran stepped inside. He was in more casual clothing than he had been at the lighthouse. He wore a teal t-shirt which matched his eyes, dark jeans and leather boots.

He moved through the pub, speaking to people, most of whom seemed happy to talk to him.

But despite his casual attire, this was still work – he had his notepad ready again, asking informal questions to the pub-goers.

Although he was maintaining a tight air of professionalism, Genny could see the hallmarks of a burnt-out man. His thumb tapped on the edge of his notepad as he waited for responses. His eyes were sunken with dark circles. He moved through the group aimlessly, as if struggling to concentrate on the case.

That was when she realised something – he had no partner with him.

Genny's partner, DS Rob Hutton, around fifteen years her junior and still finding his feet on the job, had been her right-hand man. Every caseload was a shared job, teamwork to utilise the time they spent as boots on the ground.

The partnership between DI and DS was invaluable, even with someone more inexperienced as your second. Where was Cochran's DS? Surely, he should have delegated the grunt work of questioning the locals to his subordinate, leaving his energy for the task of piecing together the clues?

She shook her head, turning back to her dinner, annoyed with herself for speculating. She had left that all behind, so why did she keep obsessing over the case?

It was hardly her business whether DI Cochran had the resources for it.

She just had to put it out of her mind, focus on doing what she could to prepare for her business to open.

And yet… as she finished her salad, her eyes trailed DI Cochran around the room, assessing his every action and wondering how she might handle the case if she had been assigned to it.

By the time Genny finished her meal and paid at the bar, DI Cochran had left, and although she couldn't shake thoughts of the case, she was comforted by the idea that he might have had a breakthrough by talking to someone and had gone home to rest.

She decided to take Pip for a walk on the beach before heading back to the inn, taking the road down by the river. It was quiet, but she could hear voices in the distance.

As she rounded the corner, she saw two figures on the bridge up ahead, bodies contorted with anger, mid-argument.

She recognised the figure on the left as she grew nearer, her blue hair shining in the light from the streetlamps – Skye Devon, furiously pointing her finger at a man in front of her. The man was in his mid-twenties, around Skye's age, with dark hair and scruffy clothes, but Genny was sure she hadn't seen him before. He hadn't been at the lighthouse opening.

He shouted something back, causing Skye to burst into hysterical tears.

They seemed to notice Genny and Pip approaching, Skye walking fast-paced over the other side of the bridge. The man nodded an awkward greeting at Genny before turning and walking back in the direction Genny had just come from.

It seemed Skye was even less popular than Imogen had made out. Whatever their reasoning, both the young man and Kristian had argued with Skye tonight, and she couldn't help but feel that the tension was linked to Mitchell's murder.

But how? And why would anyone want to kill him anyway?

Stop it, Genny, she chided herself as her and Pip scrambled down the path to the beach below the Sandhaven clifftops.

She let Pip off of her leash and walked along the shore as she excitedly zoomed off towards the sea.

"Great, you'll be filthy by the time we get back to the inn!" Genny laughed, pleased to see the dog enjoying herself. There had been limited walking spots for a highly energetic dog in London, resorting to the same few parks or catching the train out into the countryside on weekends.

Another memory surfaced, no matter how hard she tried to push it down.

"I can't believe you got a puppy," Annabelle had laughed, cuddling Pip to her. "How on earth are you going to look after a dog with your job?"

"She'll be a help, not a hinderance," Genny had shrugged, pouring another glass of wine. "Dogs are highly intelligent."

"Sure," Annabelle had conceded. "Although I'm not sure they solve murders."

"Maybe not," Genny had sighed. "But they certainly cheer you up after you have."

Genny sniffled, fighting tears as she walked across the sand.

Two years and a few hundred miles still wasn't enough. Annabelle was everywhere to her, and that fact was a comfort as much as it was a curse.

4

"I know this is a really difficult time for you all," Genny said with one hand over her heart. "I don't want to push you for an estimated completion date, but you know how it is – I've got a lot of money sunk into this and I really can't afford to delay my business' opening by too much."

Genny stood face to face with Chris Davies – a builder at Mitchell's company - outside Foxglove Cottage, which was just as it had been two days ago when she had arrived, due to Mitchell's passing. Desperate for an update, she had found an email for Chris, the second in command after Mitchell's own son, Jake, who she didn't want to disturb during his grief.

She felt awful about even asking, but she would soon be haemorrhaging money with a bank loan that would demand repayment whether she was open for business or not.

"I totally get it, please don't feel bad," Chris said earnestly. His eyes were puffy and Genny could tell he too was grieving Mitchell's death, making her feel even worse for asking. "It's business, the cogs still have to keep turning. But with Mitchell's... passing... we're a little bit all over the place as you can imagine. My plan is to hire another contracting company in, with your permission. I would fully vet them myself, I assure you."

"I'm more than happy for you to do that," Genny nodded, a little relieved that he at least had thought about their dilemma during this difficult time.

"Once the police investigation is over, and Mitchell has been buried, we'll start trying to get back to normal. But I hope you understand this was a shock to all of us, especially to his son, Jake"

"'Of course, of course," Genny nodded. "I really appreciate your honesty, Chris."

"No problem. Once I've confirmed the new company, I'll email you about a completion date."

"Thank you," Genny said. "Is there any news about the investigation? I know it's hard to have to wait to bury him until it is over, I'm sure the police are being diligent."

"It is hard. You used to be a police officer – is that right? People in town were saying it. We just really want to lay him to rest, but the family understand they need to find out who did this to him," Chris sighed, holding back emotion in his voice.

"I was, yes," Genny nodded. Word got around fast here. "I completely understand, but I'm sure DI Cochran is doing all he can to get the case solved so you can pay your respects to your friend."

"We're actually having a little bit of a memorial today – no burial of course. It's at the village green at 6pm, if you'd like to come along."

"I would, thank you," Genny said. It made sense that the community wanted to do something to honour him, even if they couldn't have an official funeral yet.

As despicable as it was, in her experience, the killers often attended these events, keeping a watchful eye on the misery they had caused.

The memorial was respectfully done. Mitchell's wife in a black dress, stood by a table filled with remembrance candles for each guest to take and hold, filling the night air with little pinpricks of light. She clutched a photo of Mitchell in her hands.

"I'm so sorry for your loss," Genny said, taking a candle and handing one each to Bev and Tom, who had come with her.

"He was a darling man," Bev said to his widow tenderly.

"Thank you," she replied, blinking away tears.

They moved from the table, finding an empty spot on the village green as Bev and Tom's friends came to talk to them.

Genny noticed DI Cochran arrive, taking a candle of his own and giving a respectful nod to Mitchell's widow. Genny remembered how it felt to stay detached on a case like this, giving very little comfort to those grieving in order to stay impartial on the case. It was not unheard of for the widow to be the culprit – in fact, statistically, Genny knew that it was more likely to be the spouse than anyone else.

That didn't make it any easier to give a nod to someone in immense pain rather than reassure them that you would hunt down the killer and bring them to justice.

DI Cochran moved through the groups, greeting people until he locked eyes with Genny.

She moved away from the Beechams and smiled at him.

"I was hoping to see you here," he said, running a hand through his hair. "I know this is not the ideal place to speak to you, but…"

Genny furrowed her eyebrows – she had no idea what he might be about to ask. Surely, he had ruled her out as a suspect by now? She had been with Tom and Bev for hours before the lighthouse re-opening.

"Go ahead," she said gently. "I won't bite."

He chuckled awkwardly, "You are no longer a suspect, naturally." Genny nodded. "You are new to the island, and you were accounted for and seen during the time period we established as the murder window – about fifteen minutes before the lighthouse re-opening."

"I'm relieved to hear it," Genny said. "Is that what you wanted to tell me?"

"No," he said, shifting his weight from one foot to the other. "Actually, I was hoping that you might have some insights into the case – professional insights, I mean. This is deeply unorthodox of me, I know, but I could really use anything you might have. From a DI to a retired DI, I know you won't have been able to help yourself but take note of the details of the case."

Genny wanted to deny the fact, but he was right. Even if she hadn't been at the place of the murder and known the victim, a case like this rippled through a community, and she couldn't help but notice potential motives and suspects.

"I'll co-operate in any way that I can," she said simply. "Although I'm not sure in which capacity I can really help you."

"Well, that's where the unorthodox part comes in," DI Cochran said, looking around covertly and placing a hand on her back to lead her further away from the others. They sat on a bench at the edge of the village green by a duck pond. He settled onto the bench, as if hoping it would anchor him down enough to get out the words. "I don't have a partner at the moment – DS Maria Moreno has just had a strapping baby girl and her maternity leave doesn't end for another five months, if she returns at all."

"Won't you be assigned another partner?" Genny asked.

"Well, that's the problem," Cochran sighed. "Solent Island is small and the crime rate is low. Our Superintendent covers all of the islands plus the Isle of Wight and some of Hampshire. She's very busy and she's warned me that she can't spare the personnel for an island which historically has been handled by a small team."

Genny felt for him – often bureaucracy got in the way of good policework.

"So, you need a second," Genny said with a slow breath.

"Yes, a sounding board, someone who knows policework, someone who knows the case," Cochran continued. "I know it is unbelievably cheeky of me to point this out, but you are sort of in between things at the moment. And it is in your best interest to solve this case as quickly as possible too."

Genny smirked – he wasn't wrong. Solving Mitchell's murder would give some much-needed closure to his family, friends and colleagues. Selfishly, that benefited her and her business.

And personally, she cared about the case. She could feel it pulling at her. She wanted to feel the pieces click into place again, like they had so many times before.

And yet… after everything with Annabelle…

"I've completely messed this up, haven't I?" Cochran asked. "I misread you, please ignore me."

"No – wait," Genny said. "You didn't."

I might regret this, she thought. *Forgive me, Annabelle.*

"I didn't?"

"No," she assured him. "I'll do it. I'll help you solve the case."

Genny fiddled with the empty sugar packet from her cup of coffee nervously.

She had arranged to meet DI Cochran the next day in a little café, *The Cup and Saucer*, on the high street of Whitebourne to discuss the case.

She wasn't sure what she was most nervous about – how unofficial this all was, or the fact that she was returning to a world she had spent so long trying to leave.

And yet… the case had not left her head since she had first seen Mitchell's body on the lighthouse steps. Every detail, every speculation was whipping around her head whether she wanted them to or not. She might as well be useful.

DI Cochran entered the café, not quite spotting her at first.

He was a few years younger than her, perhaps even a decade, thirty-five or so, but he held himself with the calm maturity of someone twice his age.

"Oh, you already have a coffee," he said with a brief nod, joining her. "Let me buy you a cake or a sandwich – anything you like, on me."

"No, I'm okay for now," Genny said. In truth she was far too anxious to eat anything.

"Sorry that this is a little… odd," he said, shuffling his chair forward. "I'm a little new to murder cases, if I'm honest."

"Your first one?"

"My first one as DI," he explained. "I had four murder cases as DS, under a man three times my age who had been in the police force all of his life. He was very good at taking charge."

"If it is any reassurance, Inspector," Genny said. "You're doing fine."

"Please, call me Remy," he insisted. "If we're going to work together, I can't have you calling me 'Inspector'. And I appreciate the assurance, but I can't help but think that my old boss would have solved this by now. We're heading towards a week since the murder, and I have no solid leads. It's like he was killed by an invisible man. No one saw anything."

"Why don't we go over what you *do* have," Genny said pointedly. "Torturing yourself with what you haven't got won't help anything. Going over old ground is nearly always the solution."

"Okay," Remy nodded, looking around the café fervently. "But perhaps we should take a walk so we can't be overheard."

"A smart idea," Genny said, finishing her coffee while Remy ordered one to go.

Pip bounded alongside them as they walked up the high street towards the coastal paths.

"Mitchell Collins, 64, general contractor running his own company, Collins and Son Building Contractors," Remy started as they took the steeper of the two coastal paths. "Next of kin was his wife now widow, Yolanda Collins, 35, and his son from his first marriage Jake Collins, 27. He and Jake worked together in the family business along with a handful of long-term employees."

"Who was his first marriage to?"

"Loretta Collins, 62. They seemed to be on good terms from what the community had to say," Remy explained.

"And the murder itself – cause of death? Shooting, I'm guessing from the wound?"

"Yes, likely with a small, handheld gun," Remy said. Just as Genny had thought.

"So, short range – whoever shot him was within a few metres of him?" Genny asked.

"Yes, although the wound you saw on his chest was actually the exit wound – it seems he was shot in the back, facing the lighthouse, and the body dragged onto the steps of the lighthouse. The bullet was found lodged in the masonry of the lighthouse entrance."

"Is that why there was so much blood on him?" Genny asked, remembering the splash of red up his chest, face and the steps around him. His red and green tartan jacket, his jeans, all soaked with red.

"Interestingly, that wasn't blood, or at least not all of it," Remy said. "It was paint."

"Paint?!"

They huffed as they reached the clifftop, the lighthouse in view, half a mile from them. They paused, looking out across the sea.

"Specifically red masonry paint, most likely from painting the lighthouse's signature red stripe," Remy replied. "The paint can was found a short way from the body, and the only prints on it were Mitchell's, Jake's and two of their employees – Chris Davies and George Chibnall. It was a local make called Dilbury's, pretty standard on the island."

"So, the killer was likely wearing gloves," Genny concluded. "The weather is still warm for September, so the gloves were intentional. The murderer planned this. But why douse him with paint? To make a statement?"

But why red paint? To make the scene look more dramatic?

"It seems that way," Remy said. "What statement exactly, I'm not sure." He sighed and looked around. "We should walk up to it, if you're willing? We can picture the scene better."

"Okay," Genny agreed. "Good idea."

They walked the rest of the path and approached the lighthouse through the wetlands.

"Tell me about Skye Devon and the SIWS – why did Kristian Nobel mention them during his speech?"

Genny asked. "I heard more about them from a woman in Whitebourne - Polly Montford-Blake?"

"Ah, 'Poisonous Polly'," Remy laughed. "She's not terribly popular either, as the nickname suggests. How did you end up speaking to her?"

His surprise seemed a high compliment to Genny and she shrugged as if to say she wasn't really sure either.

"I met her at a dog walking group. She wasn't very nice to be around, I'll admit," Genny said mirthlessly. "But she said Skye was quite a controversial figure in the community."

Remy blew out his breath reflectively and replied, "She is. Kristian Nobel hates her more than anyone, and frankly it isn't without reason."

"Because of the protesting?"

"Exactly."

"But what is it Skye and her conspirators were protesting?"

"The wetlands are a protected area," Remy explained, gesturing round at the landscape. "There are countless rare birds which nest here, not to mention voles, insects and all kinds of plants which are native to the island and in decline. No one was happy when the Nobels came onto the scene flashing their cash-"

"-Polly and her friends also mentioned that."

"They were just like all the other developers we've had come to the island at first, until they turned their attention to the lighthouse. It has a lot of history to it – first built in the 1700s and used during World War II as an outpost for the Home Guard, watching for German submarines in the waters between us and the Isle of Wight."

"Wow, I didn't know any of that," Genny remarked. No wonder it was so important to the community.

"Well, Kristian Nobel wanted to use all of that to turn it into a tourist attraction. The usual - a little café and gift shop, charge an entry fee, have a historian to take people around and tell them stories of the lighthouse."

"Sounds like a solid business idea, and great for the island."

"That's what people thought at first," he shrugged. "But the planning permission included a byway up from the main road, and a car park outside of the lighthouse. Although they wouldn't have encroached on the wetlands themselves, the SIWS argued that the construction noise and pollution would be detrimental to the Four-Ringed Plover population, who were nesting at the time."

"A fair argument," Genny nodded.

"The council approved the planning permission, and rumour has it that he bribed the councillor, but that's unsubstantiated – we looked into it. The SIWS were furious, and Skye headed up a protest, throwing cans of red paint all over the lighthouse midway through construction."

The path ended, and they continued along the grass, coming up to the lighthouse.

From the back, it was just as it had been a few days earlier, calm, peaceful; it was as if nothing had happened. The sea thrummed below them, a constant and gentle reminder that the world was continuing despite it all.

"Well, that is a very clear link to our murder," Genny said. "Either Skye or the other protestors were making another statement, or someone wants us to think they were responsible."

"I'd vote for the latter," Remy said. "Kristian Nobel insisted that Skye and the SIWS must be responsible for this murder – an attempt to ruin the opening night – but it seems a little beyond their usual pranks."

"I agree," she said, thinking carefully as they stepped across the grass surrounding the lighthouse. She looked down the cliff. "There's no byway, or car park," she realised.

"That's right," he nodded. "The protest had the desired impact. The council felt pressured to overturn their decision and Kristian Nobel had to abandon the plans. The lighthouse is now nothing more than a renovated shell with a few infographics in it. He likely won't make back any of the money he put into it."

"Then, if anything, he is the one with a motive for murder, just not a motive to murder our victim," she pointed out.

"From my experience on this job, and my experience of Mr. Nobel himself, I can't imagine him having the stomach to do something like that, let alone the ingenuity to cover the body in red paint."

"The red paint..." Genny stopped walking, deep in thought. "Was it the same red paint that was used on the lighthouse? The can that was found there? Not just red masonry paint, but the actual paint used on the lighthouse itself?"

Remy halted too. He took a moment to catch up to her line of thought. His right hand swept through his hair as he followed the thread.

"We could easily find that out," he said. "I'll contact the lab. If the paint was not the same one Mitchell Collins' company was using, we may be able to trace the origin of the paint."

"If they bought it on the island that is," Genny agreed. "If not, it could be another loose thread."

"But it's a potential lead," Remy said softly. "And goodness knows there hasn't been many of those in this case so far."

They reached the lighthouse, the police tape still around the scene, but the body and blood cleared up.

"Forensics did what they could," Remy said, leading her around to the entrance. "There were no fingerprints on any part of the lighthouse walls or the door besides Kristian, Roisin, Mitchell and Jake's."

"That's consistent with our theory that the killer was wearing gloves.

"Or…" Remy said slowly. "It means that one of those three killed him and presumed we would discount them given how circumstantial the forensic evidence is."

"The fingerprints tell us very little," she settled. "It's frustrating, but it's not the be all and end all." She regarded the outside of the building for a moment, peering inside through one of the tiny windows on the ground floor. She could make out brand new flooring, and walls lined with infographics about the lighthouse's history. "How long were Mitchell's company working on the lighthouse?"

"A few months," he replied, looking up at the iconic red stripe. "They ripped out most of the interior, which was previously a living space for the lighthouse keepers."

"Someone lived here?!"

"Yes, many generations of keepers since it was first built in the 1700s."

"But not anymore?" Genny crossed her arms and stood back, trying to imagine what it would be like to live out here, far from the rest of the island and with only the constant sound of the sea to keep you company.

"The last keeper left twenty years ago or so," Remy said. "That's what my questioning revealed, at least. No one seemed to know much about him"

Genny sighed, moving around the lighthouse. She could see where the bullet mark was in the masonry, a tiny dent that you wouldn't notice unless you knew what had happened here, a small echo of a tragedy.

"There are still so many questions in this case, which is why it is such a puzzle," she said slowly. "The chief of which is what does the lighthouse have to do with Mitchell's murder? The paint splatter, the arguments about planning permission and Kristian Nobel's finger-pointing all suggest that the murder was motivated by the lighthouse. But why? Mitchell and his team spent a few months here at most. It's hardly a reason for the protestors to kill him. He was a hired contractor, not the owner."

"I agree." Remy wiped his hands over tired eyes and paused in thought. "What if we go with your theory that it was only made to *look* as if it was to do with the lighthouse drama – the paint splatter is so blatant, the killer probably wanted it to be a distraction."

"Then we are left without any motive at all."

"There must be a motive in Mitchell's life that we've missed. Who would stand to gain from his death?" Remy shrugged. He sighed and stood back. "Let's imagine it."

He stood directly opposite the entrance and held up his hand like a gun. He repositioned himself a few times, lining up with the dent in the stone, and pretended to fire.

"Bang!" He imitated the noise and plotted the line of the bullet with his fingers.

Bang. The sound of wheels spinning and a terrible scream. Genny sprinted towards the chaos, faltering as she saw the scene in front of her.

"A planned attack," Remy said, still imagining it. "Someone who knew he would be up here at this time, getting the lighthouse ready to open while the Nobels gathered everyone for the speech. Perhaps the murderer chanced it, used a silencer during the speech itself. It's unlikely that no one would have heard him fall down, in that case."

A body, fallen down in the road, the car whizzing away into the distance. Annabelle.

"Are you okay, Genny?" Remy asked, coming back over to her. "You've gone pale."

Genny realised she hadn't been breathing as she came to reality, back to the clifftop. Pip was licking her limp fingertips reassuringly.

"Oh, I'm just tired," Genny lied, not sure she was convincing. "*The Mudlark* isn't the most comfortable venue for a good night's sleep."

Two years on and she was still terrible at hiding the flashbacks. She could only imagine how she looked to Remy in that moment, frozen and ashen on the spot as they discussed a murder case.

"Should we head back to town?" Remy asked, his eyes focussing on her with genuine worry. "I fulfil my earlier offer to get you some cake – the sugar might help with the fatigue."

"I'm okay, honestly," she insisted, waving away his kindness, taking a few steps forward and planting herself in front of the lighthouse again.

He was being thoughtful and yet she couldn't accept it without feeling she would fall apart.

"Okay," he said gently, watching her.

She attempted a reassuring smile. "Back to the case," she insisted. "I think you're right. The murder had to be planned to take place here and at that particular time. The culprit knew Mitchell would be here, and they knew he would be alone."

"That must narrow down the suspects," Remy suggested coming shoulder to shoulder with her, a look of worry still etched across his features. "The Nobels must have known he would be here, and his colleagues."

"And his family," Genny said with a click of her fingers. "You asked who stood to gain from his death – the first person we should be pointing a finger at is his wife."

"I already spoke to her," he answered. "I couldn't find a motive."

"There's always a motive amongst married couples."

"Ha!" Remy chuckled. "A thin line between love and hate?"

"In my experience, a thin line between love of a person and love of what they offer you. Money. Power. Social status. We just need to dig deeper. Let's speak to her, catch her on the backfoot – like I said before, it doesn't hurt to cover old ground again."

Get the next book in the series!

Murder at Owlwood Vicarage

A. S. McClatchie

The residents are coming together to celebrate Christmas just as new vicar Angellica Clementine is instated at Owlwood Vicarage.

But during her own Christmas party, Angellica is found dead, slumped against the big Christmas tree at the end of the garden in her red party dress and a dog collar.

Book Two – The Solent Island Mysteries

5

"Oh, the beaches look lush, I'm going to need a free holiday at your place next summer," Genny's friend Ash said with a smirk as Genny span her phone around to show her the view from the estuary of the River Whitebourne. She promised to video call as soon as she'd gotten settled, but with everything going on it had slipped her mind.

She and Ash had been friends since school, a bond that had never wavered over the years, despite their different lifestyles.

"I think everyone back home has already decided they are coming to stay here," Genny laughed. "Mum will probably move in."

"She just might do that," Ash laughed. "I saw her yesterday, actually, in the carpet shop on the King's Road."

"What on earth were you doing in a carpet shop?" Genny teased. "Don't tell me you're re-decorating *again*?"

It was a running joke that Ash – an artist and interior designer – constantly fiddled with her house. It had gotten to the point a few years ago where barely a week went by in between some sort of decorating.

"I just like looking at the carpets!" Ash answered mock-defensively. "I'm allowed to look, aren't I?"

"Just so long as you don't decide you want the living room to go from navy blue to dark teal or something," Genny grinned. She found a large driftwood log along the shore of the estuary and sat down. Pip was almost at the point where the river met the open sea, barking at the waves.

"Now you mention it, the living room carpet has never really looked right to me," Ash mused.

"Tony will move out if you keep ripping the house apart," Genny pointed out.

"Oh, he wouldn't dare!" She shot back humorously. She added with a sardonic smirk, "He knows I'd take him for everything in the divorce."

"He'd be thrilled – then you can keep all the tins of paint that you've accumulated over the years."

"All jokes aside, that's not why I was in the carpet shop," she explained. "I was there for a client when I saw your mum. We got chatting and went for a coffee down Pond Alley. We mostly talked about you, of course."

"I'm flattered," Genny grinned.

"She told me all about the issues with the cottage, although you had texted me about that already. But she also said there was a murder at a lighthouse?! You've been sending me photos of your full English every morning, but you didn't think to tell me there was a murder?!"

"It's all been a bit hectic," Genny sighed. "It was my builder who was killed."

"Wow, I'm sorry to hear that. Have the police figured out who did it yet?"

"No," she said, pursing her lips as she debated whether or not to mention her meetings with DI Remy Cochran. She made up her mind and slowly added, "Don't tell my Mum if you see her again but… I've been helping."

"With the case?" Ash asked, more than a little concern evident in her tone.

"Yeah," Genny said. "I know that... I know that I left the police for a reason, but I just... I couldn't get this case out of my head."

"Genny..." Ash cautioned. "You know I'm the last person in the world to tell you what you should or shouldn't do, but I think we all saw what you went through when Anna... well, you know. Are you sure it's such a good idea to get involved in a murder case?"

"I feel like I need to," she replied. "If I'm honest, I think if I didn't take the DI up on his offer my head might explode trying to imagine all the possible scenarios."

"You were always like that – you could never concentrate on anything else until the case was solved," Ash gave a half-smile. "Just please promise me you'll look after yourself?"

"Of course," Genny smiled. "Don't worry about me, really. I have Pip by my side and the DI is a good guy. I'm sure we will solve the case soon and then I can move onto my bakery."

"You deserve that fresh start, Gen," Ash smiled. "Don't get out of your depth."

They said their goodbyes and hung up the call as Genny headed back up towards *The Mudlark*. Remy was due to pick her up at 9am to go over to the Collins' house.

In truth, she was a little worried that they might not solve the case by the time the cottage and bakery were ready. Despite their conversation the day before, Genny hadn't moved any closer to a breakthrough overnight. The motives, the location, and the method of the murder were somehow all out of line with what they knew about Mitchell.

Remy picked her up in an unmarked car and they drove twenty minutes across woodland roads to the nearby town of Market Yaxley, where the Collins' lived.

The house was grand, much grander than Genny had been expecting. Mitchell may have owned his own company and turned a good profit, but this house nodded to more than that.

The front garden was gated, and Remy got out to press the intercom to be let in, someone inside pressing a switch to pull the gates aside.

The house itself was probably worth a couple of million, with space for six or seven bedrooms, a double garage and swimming pool in the back garden.

"This is not what I was expecting," Genny said, looking to Remy for his reaction.

"That's what I thought last time I came here," he said. "But it is conceivable that he worked hard and managed his money well. He was the most popular contractor on the island after all."

"You're right, it's possible. But even if you have this much wealth, wanting to *show* it like this... that's another thing. I saw plenty of wealthy people in London who lived in fairly unassuming houses. Nice houses, yes. Big houses, sure. But not like this."

"Hm, that's a good point." Remy parked up and turned off the car. From their position they could see the garden and the full-length pool. A hot tub sat at one end of the garden as well. "Are you suggesting that he wanted people to see how well the company were doing? To rub it in somehow?"

"Perhaps it wasn't him that wanted to show off," Genny answered, gesturing with a nod of her head as a woman opened the front door.

It was Yolanda, Mitchell's second wife. Genny remembered her from the memorial.

"She is a lot younger than him," Remy nodded. "But why murder him when she clearly had access to his money already?"

"Never underestimate the hold money can have over someone. She might have convinced him to turn the house into an L.A mansion, but if he still held the purse strings, that's reason enough."

They exited the car and greeted Yolanda at the door as she led them through to the living room.

"Would you like a drink, Inspector?" She said, eyeing Genny with a confused smile.

Remy had assured her that she was able to be present for these informal conversations, but she could see the tension her attendance was causing. She wasn't part of the police anymore, and to the people of Solent Island, she was little more than a stranger. Worse than that, she was an outsider, a mainlander who had barely got her feet on the ground yet.

She took a grounding breath as they sat down on an uncomfortable but lavish loveseat.

The house's interior was modern, with sleek lines and minimalist décor, filled with sunlight from large windows which overlooked the pool. The lawn was bright green, and sprinklers hissed periodically in the background.

"No drink for me, thank you," Remy answered.

"And… you?" Yolanda asked Genny.

"No, no, that's okay, thank you," Genny said.

"Okay," Yolanda nodded, perching on a gold-patterned white chair. "I'm not sure what more I can tell you that I haven't already," she said cagily.

She looked tired, with no make-up and in a pair of jogging bottoms and a t-shirt. From the design of the house, Genny was sure that she was someone who dressed formally every day, even just at home.

"I appreciate this is difficult," Remy said gently. "But sometimes we have to return to old lines of questioning to develop a fuller picture of the events."

He was good at that – formulating the official lines. Genny had been too, once upon a time. She knew the words to avoid – 'victim', 'murder', 'tragedy'. Nothing too emotional, otherwise your suspect might become uncontrollable. You needed everything to stay as close to neutral as possible until the moment that you needed to push for more.

Voices from outside turned their heads and the glass back doors opened – an older woman and a young man entered. Genny instantly recognised the young man – he had been arguing in the road with Skye Devon.

"Jake, Loretta, the Inspector has some more questions," Yolanda explained.

Jake. So, it was Mitchell's son that had been arguing with Skye Devon. But what about? They had seemed familiar with each other, passionate almost.

And Loretta, Mitchell's ex-wife too. She was wiry and slender, but held herself with an air of entitlement, a confidence which could only come with age and wealth.

Genny was surprised to see them all in one place; she couldn't imagine the family dynamic of a man remarrying someone only a few years older than his son.

"And this is my... colleague, Genny Hadley," Remy explained, only hesitating slightly on the word 'colleague'. They didn't seem to notice.

Jake and Loretta, like Yolanda, were distraught in their grief, both looking exhausted.

"We're happy to assist the investigation in any way we can, aren't we, Jake?" Loretta said, taking the sofa opposite Remy and Genny.

Jake shrugged and sat on another chair, nearer to Yolanda.

"So, Yolanda," Remy said slowly, "How long had you and Mitchell been married?"

"About six years," she answered with a tearful shrug, pulling at the sleeve of her t-shirt absent-mindedly. "It would have been seven in the summer."

"And how did you meet?" Remy continued.

Yolanda and Loretta shared an awkward look.

"We met at the cycling club," she explained. "Mitchell often went up there with his friend Paul, who is a member, and I went up there with my husband at the time."

"So, you were married when you first met Mitchell?" Genny asked, leaning forward on the seat.

"They were both married," Loretta interjected quickly with an eye roll. "Is this really relevant to what happened to Mitchell, Inspector?" She added, ignoring Genny and directing her question to Remy only.

"It could be," he stressed. "Please just answer our questions as best you can."

Loretta crossed her arms and sank back into the sofa.

"Yes, we were both married," Yolanda said. "But it's not what you think - we didn't have an affair. Our marriages ended and we… found each other."

"And it was a happy marriage?" Remy asked. He kept his face blank, showing an expert level of restraint.

"Of course!" Yolanda yelped, sniffling into a tissue that she pulled from a geometric glass tissue holder on the side table. "What are you implying?"

"We're not implying anything," Genny quickly jumped in. "The details are important."

"Well, it was happy. Very happy. I know what you must be thinking," Yolanda sobbed. "A much younger woman, second marriage – you think I must have been a gold digger!"

"No," Remy said. "But the question of inheritance is important. Who stands to inherit this beautiful house?"

The three interviewees looked at each other, as if deciding whether or not to be honest.

"Well, the Inspector can pull the information through the police reports anyway," Genny shrugged, hoping to smoke them out. "I guess then we'll have our answer…"

"Yolanda and I were equal beneficiaries," Jake said, speaking for the first time since they had arrived.

"That was good of your Dad," Genny said, deciding to push Jake a little further. "Does that mean you will get half of the sale of the house?"

"Sale?" Yolanda said suddenly.

"I'm sorry," Genny pretended to have made a mistake. "I just presumed that Jake might want to sell his half."

"Well, now that you mention it…" Jake said hesitantly.

"You can't!" Yolanda screeched. "It's our home! It was Mitchell's home!"

"So, what's the alternative? I continue to live with my stepmother who is only ten years older than me?" Jake snorted derisively.

Genny and Remy shared a look.

"Let's all cool off," Genny said. "I think we have what we need for now."

Jake stormed off outside again, and Yolanda ran upstairs in a flood of tears, leaving Loretta awkwardly perched on the sofa.

"I'll show you out," she said. "Excuse us, we're all grieving."

"It's completely understandable," Remy said. "We're sorry to have to keep bothering you."

"Just so long as you find my ex-husband's killer," Loretta said, leading them back to the front door. "Jake is immature, and Yolanda is heartbroken, but I'm incensed. I won't rest until Mitchell's killer is behind bars."

"Neither will we," Genny assured her.

With a final nod, she showed them out, closing the door behind them.

"Well, that was illuminating," Genny said as they climbed back into Remy's car.

"Very," Remy said, pausing before starting the engine. "You were very impressive in there."

"Me?" Genny chuckled. "What did I do?"

"You pushed them," Remy said. "Yes, they imploded on themselves, but you just got us a motive for murder – money. Jake certainly seems to gain the most – a fortune and independence from his stepmother and mother – plus witnesses told me that he and his father often argued."

"I've been told the same," Genny nodded.

"I'm going to head to the station after I drop you off. I'll see what else I can dig up on him," Remy said. "It's going to be a little difficult to prove that he wasn't where he claimed to be at the time of the murder."

"Which was?"

"Up a ladder in your loft," he sighed. "He claims his Dad had already left for the lighthouse, and the others clocked off early. He was there alone."

"Perhaps his weak alibi can work to our advantage. If no one can corroborate his story of being at Foxglove Cottage, there's no reason why he couldn't have gone up to the lighthouse to commit the murder."

"I'll let you know if I find anything else," Remy said, starting the car engine. "In the meantime, we should speak to someone else, see what more was hidden from me initially."

"I had a thought, actually," Genny said as they left the driveway, the metal gates, clanking shut behind them automatically. "I recognised Jake, and not from my cottage."

"Oh? Did you see him at the lighthouse re-opening?"

"No – I saw him and Skye Devon arguing outside *The Water's Edge* the day after the murder. At first it seemed as if she was angry with him for something, but as it grew more heated, she burst into tears and stormed away."

"How strange," Remy said, quiet in thought for a moment. "They were just in the street?"

"Yes," Genny pondered. "By the bridge."

"Did anyone else see them?"

"I don't think so," she shrugged. "I couldn't make out anything they were saying, and it was dark, so I wasn't sure who they were to begin with. I wonder if they were conspirators – an 'I scratch your back, you scratch mine' situation?"

"You mean, Skye helps Jake kill Mitchell and Jake helps her…"

"To kill Kristian, perhaps?" Genny suggested. "But that doesn't make sense – the red paint was clearly supposed to make us think it was Skye. Why would they implicate themselves like that?"

"Far too conceited to be a double bluff," Remy mused. "Knowing Skye, her emotions run a little high. Perhaps they were arguing about something mundane and it got heated?"

"Maybe. But I think we should speak to her anyway – see what she knows about Jake Collins."

"Good idea," Remy nodded. "Tomorrow. She shouldn't be too hard to track down."

"Okay," Genny agreed.

6

"Are you eating enough? You look skinny," Genny's mother bleated over the video call.

"Mum, I can only see your nose, hold the phone further away from your face," Genny grinned. "And yes, I'm eating."

She was sat in the back garden of *The Mudlark* with a cup of coffee in hand, enjoying the view of the swans on the river.

"Is this better?" Her mum asked, holding the phone at an awkward angle with both hands.

"It'll do, Mum," Genny replied with a small smile.

"Ash told me you've started helping out on this murder case at the lighthouse," her mum said.

Damn it, Ash, Genny thought.

"She wasn't supposed to tell you that," she groaned.

"Well, I'm glad she did. We're both worried about you."

"I'm fine, I promise. I told her that I wouldn't be able to get the case out of my head otherwise. I'm doing this in a healthy way, I promise. The DI is doing all the work, I'm just helping him put the puzzle pieces into place."

"I think you need a hobby," her mum persisted. "Take up tennis instead of all this murder business. Work on your recipes for when the bakery opens."

"I don't have a kitchen at the moment, Mum," Genny laughed.

"Well then… rambling. Or knitting. I find it very therapeutic."

"Mum, I'm okay, I swear. I wouldn't undo all the work I've done over the past two years by risking it, I promise. I'm being healthy about this."

"Fine," her mum said, unconvinced. "How is the cottage coming along?"

"The substitute contractors have made some progress, but they say it will still be a while longer. Another week, maybe."

"Well, that's not too far away, I suppose," her mum smiled.

"Genny!" Bev's voice came from the guest lounge. "There's a man here for you!"

"A man?!" Genny's mum laughed salaciously. "It sounds like you already have a hobby."

"No, Mum, it's DI Cochran," Genny explained. "The man in charge of the murder case."

"Oh," her mum replied, her excitement dropping. "Just be safe my darling. I worry about you."

"I'm doing great, Mum, please stop worrying. And tell Ash not to worry either."

"I will," her Mum replied.

"Oh, sorry," Remy said as he came out of the back door of the inn. "I didn't mean to interrupt your call."

"Is that him?!" Her mum laughed. "Oh, he's dishy. Now I understand why you're helping…"

"Mum! I really have to go! Speak later!"

She hung up the call before she could say anything else inappropriate.

"I'm so sorry if you heard that," Genny said to Remy, flushing a little pink.

He smirked, "I promise that I wasn't listening."

"Good," Genny sighed. "Are we heading out?"

"Ready when you are," Remy said as she stood up. He added with a cheeky air, "It's been a while since I heard someone say the word 'dishy'."

"So, did you find out where Skye Devon lives?" Genny asked as they walked through Whitebourne at a brisk pace.

"No, but I don't need to know where she lives to find her," Remy said knowingly. "First, we've got to speak to Jake Collins again – I found out some things while I was looking up his background information at the station."

"Oh?"

"He is in debt. Pretty badly too - £40,000."

"Wow! How did he get £40,000 into debt?!"

"Loans with dodgy websites," Remy explained. "It seems Jake likes to live beyond his means. I have witness reports saying he drives a sports car and holidays in five-star hotels in Cherbourg. He apparently flashes the cash around Market Yaxley too."

"Are we going back to their house?" Genny asked as they set off on foot.

"One of my informants in the village texted me half an hour ago to say that Jake is currently knocking back more than a few drinks in *The Water's Edge*."

They found Jake just as described, hunched over the bar top with a half-drunk beer in hand.

"Jake, it's barely lunchtime," the barman said firmly. "I'm not serving you your fifth pint already."

"Don't people have any respect for grieving people anymore?" Jake said, slamming the money down onto a beermat, spraying little droplets of beer everywhere.

"Jake, we're all sorry about your Dad, but drinking isn't going to make you feel better," the barman said with a sigh, pushing the money back towards him. "I'm going to get you a water."

Genny and Remy approached.

"Oh, not you again," Jake groaned, much chattier with a few drinks in him. "Haven't you grilled me enough? I didn't kill my dad! There, I said it!"

"No?" Genny said, deciding with a nod at Remy to go in firm. "Even if his death meant you could pay off your debts?"

"What?" Jake bristled. "How do you know about those?"

"I accessed your financial information, Jake," Remy said calmly. "You are in serious trouble. Some of your demands are long overdue."

"Yeah, alright, I know how this looks," Jake slurred, finishing the pint of beer. "But that's not how it is."

"Tell us how it is," Genny said, crossing her arms. "We want to know."

"My Dad was bailing me out, alright?" Jake said with widened eyes. "He was working all these crazy jobs – the lighthouse and the cottage – and adding extra charges to people's bills so that he could pay off my debts."

Genny met Remy's eyes as they both realised the truth.

Despite her poison tongue, Polly Montford-Blake had been right about Mitchell's recent business practices, she had just been wrong about the reasoning.

"And I bet you argued about that sometimes, didn't you?" Genny pushed.

"Of course," Jake shrugged. "Dad was so mad at me when he found out I'd been borrowing all that money to buy stuff. He said I was ruining my life for temporary fun. He was right, but I was too far into it by that point. Anyway, what reason would I have to kill the man who was bailing me out?"

He was right. The story added up and it was easily provable with Jake's bank statements.

"If you inherited his money, you could pay it off all at once," she asserted. "You wouldn't need your dad to keep bailing you out, making you feel small and like a failure. Isn't that enough of a reason?"

She was determined to see through the line of questioning, but she already knew he didn't do it.

He sobbed, resting his forehead on the bar top. Genny looked at Remy, worried she'd gone too far.

Jake lifted his head back up and gave a heartfelt groan.

"I loved him, okay?" Jake mumbled through the tears. "He was my dad and I loved him, I could never kill him. Inheriting his money means nothing to me. Yolanda can have every penny for all I care. I'm already bankrupt."

"Don't think like that, Jakey," the barman said with an affectionate pat on his hand. "You're going to make your ol' man proud by running his business now. You're going to sort out your money situation and you're going to be just fine. You're going to keep his memory going, lad."

Jake sniffled and nodded.

"I don't think we've met," Genny said, reaching a hand over the bar to shake his hand.

"Perry Carter," the barman replied. "I own the place."

"Nice to meet you, Perry." She regarded him for a moment. He was sweet with Jake. The islanders were friendly and familiar with each other in general, but something about the physical touch and motivational words told her there was more to it. "Did you know Mitchell, Perry?"

"Yeah, for… oh… must be decades since I first met him," he shrugged. "Thirty years or more. He was a great man."

"He's my godfather," Jake muttered.

"And I worked for Mitchell for a while in my 20s," Perry explained. "Just a bit of painting and decorating, nothing major."

Genny nodded slowly. Remy's mobile beeped and he pulled it out of his pocket, turning away from the conversation.

"And you didn't stay in the line of work? It's pretty much chalk and cheese between that and running a pub," she asked.

"It was just a stopgap," he said with a shrug. "I spent most of my time doing runs to Dilbury's."

A lightbulb went off in Genny's head. That was the name of the brand on the paint can they'd found at the crime scene.

"Dilbury's?" She asked cooly.

"It's a building merchant on the outskirts of *hick* Market Yaxley," Jake slurred, interrupted by hiccups. Perry pushed the glass of water towards him, but he didn't seem to notice. "Dad used them for everything. Pretty much the only place you can get building supplies on the island because of *hick* importing costs."

"Right," Genny nodded, making a mental note of that.

She saw Remy was still distracted by his phone. She thanked the pair for their time and turned away as Perry gently tried again to encourage Jake to drink the water.

"Is it about the case?" Genny asked Remy in a hushed voice.

He showed his phone – a notification had popped up.

The Earthchildren have just gone live on InstaPost, click to watch now!

"That's Skye," Remy clarified.

"Skye?" Jake perked up. "Did she mention me?"

"What do you mean?" Genny asked him, pretending not to understand his interest.

"Did she text you?" Jake ignored Genny's question, getting to his feet and striding towards Remy. "What did she say?"

"No, Jake, it's just her InstaPost. She's at a protest now," Remy answered calmy, putting a hand on his shoulder placatingly. "Why do you ask?"

"We had a big fight," Jake said. "She broke up with me."

That's why they had been arguing – they were a couple, or they had been.

"She was your girlfriend?"

"Yeah, for a while now," Jake said. "But that's all over. She found out about my debts and all the things I'd spent money on. She was so angry with me. So, I told her to get the heck out of my life if she couldn't handle it. Then she ran off crying. I haven't heard from her since then."

They left Jake to wallow, heading out of the pub.

"That all tied up," Genny shrugged. "We really thought we had something."

"I agree, it's not him," Remy said. "But look."

He opened the notification on his phone and a live video started playing.

"WE WON'T GO! HEAR OUR VOICES! NO MORE HOUSES!" Skye was holding up a sign, stood in front of a field with a few other people.

"Where is that?" Genny asked.

"Hey! Hey!" Someone shouted on the video. It was Kristian Nobel, appearing from the right-hand side of the screen, getting up close to Skye as he threatened her. "I'm calling the police and you better hope that they restrain me too, you jumped up little moron!"

"Dad!" Roisin was on hand to stand in between them as the arguing continued, the other protestors continuing to chant.

"It's Peartree Acres," Remy explained. "A parcel of land that Kristian bought to build 200 houses on. Various groups stepped in to stop him."

Polly had told Genny about that. But she had also told her that The Solent Island Preservation Society had stopped the plans. So why were they protesting?

They walked to Remy's car and drove to Peartree Acres, arriving just as the police did.

Kristian's temper was flaring, and Genny didn't like how close he was getting to Skye.

Luckily, Remy had also spotted it, grabbing some handcuffs from his car and springing out.

"Calm down, Kristian!" He shouted, but the arguing and chanting was too loud.

Skye said something with a vindictive look on her face, and without hesitation, Kristian swung for her, only narrowly missing and slamming his fist into the fence post behind her head.

Skye gasped and moved forward, pulling something from her pocket – a bottle of red paint. As Kristian pulled his fist back, groaning in pain and rubbing his knuckles, Skye took aim. She squirted the bottle with propellant force, soaking his face with the paint.

He sputtered and went for her again.

"Woah, woah, that's enough!" Remy said, grabbing Kristian's arms and pulling them behind his back. "Kristian Nobel, you are under arrest for attempted assault."

"Me?! What about all of these protestors? I'm covered in paint!" Kristian bellowed. "You'll regret this, Inspector!"

"Officers – get him back to the station for processing please."

The police officers took over, clearing away the protestors and taking Kristian off in a police car, still dripping red down the front of his suit. Roisin was nowhere to be seen.

"Are you okay?" Genny asked.

"I'm fine," Remy assured her, taking a café napkin from his pocket to wipe some paint from the sleeve of his shirt. "Nothing a good dry cleaner can't fix."

The protestors started to scatter, signs hung at their sides dejectedly, but Genny managed to catch Skye, who had started to walk away with the paint bottle still in her hand.

"Skye Devon?" She asked.

"Who wants to know?" Skye asked, crossing her arms defiantly. "I don't talk to reporters for free. If you want to write about me, it'll cost you."

"No, I'm with the police," Genny clarified, Skye's expression changing to one of hatred.

"Ah, the pigs," she scoffed. "What do you want? We were protesting legally, you know. It's our right to do that."

"I know," Genny said, practicing keeping her cool like Remy. "It's actually about the murder of Mitchell Collins."

"What?!" Skye said, a flash of horror crossing her face. "Why would you think I had anything to do with that?"

"We don't know for sure that you did," Genny said. "But asking you some questions could help us catch his killer."

"I barely knew the man," Skye shrugged. "He was just some builder from a posh house in Market Yaxley."

She flipped her blue hair back from her face and pursed her lips.

She was lying.

"We know you were dating Jake Collins," Genny said, watching Skye instantly soften. "You're not in any trouble Skye, we just need to know what you know."

Her body language changed from defensive to vulnerable. Despite their argument outside *The Water's Edge*, it seemed there was real affection there.

"About Jake?" Skye said quietly. "He's not responsible for this."

"Maybe not," Genny said. "But what you know about him and his Dad could lead us to the real killer."

"Everyone liked Mitchell," Skye shrugged. "He was easy to talk to and he cared about his family, even if he and Jake did argue sometimes."

"About his debts?"

"Yeah," Skye admitted. "About his debts. But he was helping Jake to sort those out. When he found out… he was so mad. Jake moved in with me for a few days to get away from the shouting. But Mitchell came around, promised to help him get his life together."

"And Jake was helping his Dad with the lighthouse?"

"They took on the project for some extra cash – Kristian paid pretty well."

"That must have been a source of tension between you and Jake, given your protests," Genny suggested.

"It was," Skye admitted. "He was upset when I protested the car park plans – said that someone had to do the work and wouldn't it be better if it was his Dad's company so that they could get the money? But I couldn't see it like that – the lighthouse renovations posed a real threat to the local wildlife."

"So, you continued your protests and he continued to take money from Kristian Nobel. That must have been hard."

"Nearly impossible," Skye nodded slowly. "It all came to a head after his Dad was killed, and I ended things."

"Did you want to end things with him?" Genny asked gently.

"No," Skye admitted, biting her lip to try and halt the tears. "But I couldn't see any way forward. We're just so different. And he's changed since his Dad died."

"He's grieving," Genny offered. "That changes people."

Skye didn't reply, clearing her throat and trying to compose herself, her thumb tapping against the side of the paint bottle anxiously.

"Is that the same paint you used in the lighthouse protests?" Genny asked softly.

Skye looked down at the bottle.

"Yes," she admitted. "Kristian Nobel is so dramatic. It's just an eco-friendly chalk-based paint. It washes off with water."

Genny looked at the label – Mistress Shadow's EcoLife.

"Still, you can see why he was upset. What you did at the lighthouse was technically vandalism."

"It made a statement," she replied tersely. "That's all that matters."

"And spraying paint in his face today?"

"He was going to punch me! You saw!" She said indignantly.

"And you retaliated."

"This island really has gone down the pan if defending yourself against an attempted assault is worse than the initial crime," she countered.

Genny sighed. It wasn't a defence, it was revenge. They both knew that. The difference was minimal, and she was lucky that the police weren't going to arrest her too.

"Genny?" Remy approached.

"I think we've got all the information we need, Skye," Genny said. "Thank you for your time."

They headed back to the car.

"Anything?" Remy asked hopefully.

"Just more confirmation that Jake is not our killer. Whatever family tensions we've picked up on, I don't think they explain the murder."

"Back to square one," Remy sighed. "I've got paperwork for Kristian's arrest, though I'm sure he'll spend no more than a few hours in our cells before his daughter bails him out."

"That's frustrating," Genny sighed.

"Although," Remy added. "The lab just called while you were talking to Skye. I found out some more about the paint – the lab were able to confirm that it was not the same paint used on the lighthouse. Not Dilbury's. In fact, it wasn't even the same shade of red, or masonry paint as we had initially thought. It was actually chalk-based acrylic. The sort you use for painting pictures."

"Really?" Her mind started to whir. "The paint Skye uses was chalk-based."

"That's interesting," he said, his eyes scanning the treeline behind them as he thought. "But surely we've ruled her out."

"I think so," Genny nodded. "But it's more evidence for our theory that someone was trying to copy

Skye's MO. They wanted us to draw that link. It also confirms that it wasn't spur of the moment. Someone had to buy that paint and take it up there with them."

"Maybe," he said. "But I can't think how we will prove that without randomly searching suspects' houses. And even on this tiny island getting a search warrant without a concrete lead is not easy."

Genny thought for a moment.

She knew there had to be another way.

"Leave it with me," she told him. "I'll think of a way to sort this."

"Okay. I'll drop you back at the inn on the way back to the station.

The streets of Whitebourne were quiet as the sun was starting to set. Genny had decided to take Pip for a walk past Foxglove Cottage, in the hopes that her home and business might be ready soon. From the outside, she could still see work to be done inside.

She stopped and admired it, trying to imagine what she had first seen when she had found it on the estate agent's website. The history of the place had appealed to her most – generations of bakers, starting with an unmarried woman, Josephine Seabridge, in 1844, who had borrowed money from her father, the local pastor, to set up the bakery, after locals had complimented the cakes she made for church events. She had faced no end of backlash – she was effectively a spinster, and the community saw her as a pariah. That was until she opened. The cakes flew from the shelves, and with each passing year her talent and success grew until the Whitebourne bakery was famous across the island.

Josephine eventually married aged 35 to the town's chief steelworker and had one daughter, who inherited, ran and passed on the bakery.

The history had caught Genny's attention as much as the beautiful old building, but she hadn't realised how extensive the renovations would be until she visited earlier in the summer.

"Oh my goodness – you're my new neighbour, aren't you!" A voice trilled from behind Genny.

She swung around to see a woman ten or so years older than her stood in the front garden of the house next door. She had wavy brown hair, pinned up into a claw clip, and was wearing a green turtleneck jumper which accentuated how long her features were.

"I guess so," Genny smiled.

"I've heard a lot about you since you arrived," the woman said, opening the gate of her front garden and coming out onto the pavement. "I'm Pearl Linman. I'm sure you'll meet my husband, Saul, soon enough."

"Nice to meet you," Genny said. "I'm-"

"-Like I say, I know all about you," Pearl interrupted, tittering to herself. "You are the talk of Whitebourne. People are saying that you used to be a detective with the police."

"Yes," Genny replied simply, wondering what exactly people had been saying about her.

"Oh, don't look so worried," Pearl giggled. "Gossip moves fast on a small island like this, but it's harmless. Everyone was just very excited to see you helping out with the murder case. Terrible business.

DI Cochran should be glad to have a more experienced pair of hands on the team."

"DI Cochran is more than capable of solving the case without me," Genny said firmly. "I was just at a loose end and thought I'd put myself to use."

"Oh, of course, of course," Pearl cooed. "I just meant because you are older than him, and besides, I'm sure there were far more murders in London than here."

"Crime is worse in the city," Genny agreed. "But I think that has more to do with population density than anything else."

"Of course," Pearl nodded with a condescendingly bright smile. "But I'm not surprised that this murder took place here."

"How so?" Genny crossed her arms.

"Well, that lighthouse has caused nothing but trouble during its lifetime. Countless deaths backs in the 1800s, or so they say," she said. "Not to mention the accident twenty years ago."

"Accident?" Genny asked.

The lighthouse had been closed for twenty years, supposedly due to the last lighthouse keeper leaving. She hadn't presumed that there was more to the story than that.

"A boat crashed," Pearl said with a dismissive wave of her hand. "I can't remember exactly what happened after that, but I know that the lighthouse was closed pretty soon after that."

"And that was the reason?"

"That's what I heard, but I don't know any more about it," Pearl admitted. "I was not surprised when I heard that it was Mitchell who was murdered, either."

"Why not?" Genny asked. "I've heard that he was well liked in the community."

"In the community, I'm sure, but there were issues in his family."

"His son, Jake? We've already spoken to him," Genny suggested.

"No, not Jake," Pearl said, coming close and looking around as if someone might be listening in. "That new wife of his, the young one. They didn't have a happy marriage, despite Mitchell splitting with poor Loretta in order to marry her."

"What makes you think that?" Genny asked. "It is hard to judge someone else's marriage from the outside."

"It is easy to judge when you see one of the spouses out with another person," Pearl grinned salaciously. "I told Loretta – when a marriage begins with cheating, it always ends with cheating."

"You think Mitchell was cheating on his wife?"

"No," Pearl laughed. "Although that wouldn't surprise me. It was Yolanda, and what's worse, she cheated with Mitchell's best friend, Paul."

Genny remembered what Yolanda had told her and Remy: *We met at the cycling club, Mitchell often went up there with his friend Paul.*

"You've seen them together?" Genny asked, surprised. She had been so sure that Yolanda was the heartbroken widow she had made out to be.

"Better than that – I have video footage," Pearl giggled, opening a home security app on her mobile phone.

The camera faced out of Pearl's front window, towards the street.

The video footage played – Yolanda and a man with strawberry blonde hair walking down towards the river.

It was innocent enough at first. They were side by side but not touching, talking quietly back and forth, too quietly to hear what they were saying.

When they were nearly out of view of Pearl's camera, near to Genny's cottage, Yolanda turned to face Paul. He ran a finger tenderly down her cheek and then cupped her chin before leaning in to kiss her.

They broke apart a few moments later, Yolanda looking around with a worried look, but Paul laughed her worry off. They continued down the street, out of view.

"See?" Pearl twittered. "She was with Mitchell for the money, I always said that to Loretta. She put in all the hard years, supported him when his business was just a one-man operation and they could barely afford nappies for Jake, and then he turned around and betrayed her for a skank like that."

Genny hummed disapprovingly. How had she misjudged Yolanda's grief so much? It had felt so real.

"Well, that's very interesting," Genny said. "Thank you. I think it would be best if you turned your camera over to DI Cochran in the morning."

"Pardon?! Why on earth would I do that?" Pearl huffed.

"Well, I don't think you would want to withhold evidence from a murder investigation," Genny pointed out. "Plus, it is illegal to record more than your own property. I'm sure DI Cochran would hate to have to give you a fine and a blot on your record."

Pearl's face contorted in horror.

"No!" She stammered.

"I'm sure he won't, if you come with me to the police station tomorrow and show him what you showed me," Genny assured her.

"Fine," Pearl said.

Genny was unable to keep back slight smirk of satisfaction.

"Thank you."

"If DI Cochran has time to see me, of course," Pearl said pointedly. She was clearly not one to let someone else have the final word.

"I'm sure he will."

"Maybe not – I hear it was a busy day at the station."

"Oh?" Genny queried, watching Pearl closely. She had the puffed-out chest of a gossip with information.

"I hear that Kristian Nobel was arrested up at Peartree Acres. Maureen Glover lives opposite the station. She saw him being hurried inside dripping in blood."

"It was paint," Genny assured her. "He was arrested at the protest."

"Ah, Skye Devon and her nasty lot of good-for-nothings?"

"I believe it was a group calling themselves The Earthchildren."

"Yes, that's them," Pearl grumbled. "Did you hear that they put toilet paper all over the town? And then the paint at the lighthouse! And now this! Who do they think they are? Who do they think will clean up all their messes?!"

Genny nodded silently, watching Pearl get more and more angry.

"The paint was apparently easily washable," she offered, seeing that the assertion made Pearl even more annoyed.

"No doubt she stole it from that horrible little hippie shop she works in," Pearl said with a firm shake of her head.

"Hippie shop?"

"In Westmarsh," Pearl answered. "It's called *Devil's Wares* or something equally horrible. Run by some witch."

"A witch?"

"That's what they say," Pearl nodded, completely serious in her assertion.

Despite the strangeness of Pearl's information, it was a lead to follow that she didn't need Remy for.

"Well, thank you," Genny said. "I should be getting back to the inn now. It was nice to meet you. See you tomorrow."

"Yes," Pearl said sulkily. "I'll see you tomorrow."

The last thing she needed was a nosey neighbour recording her property and spreading gossip around the island about her, although she had to admit the footage of Yolanda and Paul was very compelling.

But she would need Remy's help pulling on that thread.

For now, she could follow up on the paint herself.

7

Genny took Pip back to the inn before taking a bus out to Westmarsh as the evening drew in. She knew she wouldn't have long to find the shop if she hoped to speak to the owner before it closed.

Luckily, Westmarsh high street contained very few shops.

A bakery stood at one end, next to an old schoolhouse which had been turned into a hotel. Further along was a public park, and then an estate agent.

At the end of the high street was a charity clothes shop, a candle-making shop and a café.

She was about to give up, when she noticed the sign of the café – a wiccan symbol with horns like a devil. Underneath were the word's *Witchy Wares and Café*.

She entered the café and a bored teenager behind the counter put down her phone.

"Sorry to bother you," Genny said. "I'm looking for a shop? Eco-friendly things?"

"Upstairs," the girl said, gesturing vaguely to a spiral staircase at the back of the café. "Mistress Shadow is about to close up though."

Mistress Shadow...

"Thank you," Genny said, trying to keep a straight face as she took the stairs at the back of the café up to the next level.

She was immediately hit with the smell of incense.

The shop was cluttered with objects from gemstones to witches' brooms to bags of dried herbs. Sunlight streamed in from a large paned window at one end, illuminating a counter where an elderly lady was hunched, writing in a ledger book.

This had to be Mistress Shadow, the witch Pearl had been talking about.

"Hello?" Genny asked gently. "Are you Mistress Shadow?"

"Ah, yes. But you can just call me Patty," the woman said, not looking up from the notebook. "You're here about Skye."

"Uh... yes," Genny said, a little taken aback. "How did you know that?"

The woman looked up from the book with an irreverent grin on her face.

"Even witches have social media, dear," she said. "The video of Kristian Nobel's arrest has gone viral, and you're in it."

"Oh," Genny said. Her cheeks coloured. She should know better than to assume witchcraft when it could simply be gossip. "You saw that?"

"Everyone on the island did," Patty said with a nod. "It makes sense that you're here to learn more about Skye. I am happy to tell you anything you want to know."

"I appreciate your openness," Genny said earnestly.

"Tea?" Patty asked, and on seeing Genny's hesitance, she added, "Just English Breakfast, nothing magical I promise."

"Thank you," Genny said, feeling a little silly again. "I would like that."

Patty descended the stairs to the café and came back up with two mugs of tea, handing one to Genny before taking a seat in one of two armchairs in the corner of the store. She gestured for Genny to do the same.

"What would you like to know?" She asked.

Genny sipped the tea and thought about the paint. It had clearly come from the shop, although Pearl's assumption that Skye was stealing it seemed a little unfair.

"My neighbour said that Skye works here."

"Who is your neighbour?"

"Pearl Linman."

"Ah." She nodded knowingly, sipping her tea. "Is that why you're so wary of me? Pearl told you I was some devil-worshipping heathen?"

"Well…" Genny couldn't help but say.

"Pearl and I went to school together," Patty clarified. "She's always been a little… paranoid. I had a black cat and sold herbal remedies and quickly people called me a witch. This was in the 70s, you see. People were a little less accepting then. Anyway, I decided to give them something to talk about. If they think I'm a witch, why not become 'Mistress

Shadow' and set up my cosy little shop? I've done quite well for myself and made a nice community out of the more alternative people on the island."

It was a surprisingly heartwarming story. She couldn't help but feel a little foolish for jumping to so many conclusions, especially based on the words of someone like Pearl, an obvious busybody.

"I think that's wonderful, actually," Genny said. "And Skye?"

"She works here, just as Pearl said," Patty explained. "She has done for a few years now, ever since she finished university on the mainland. She's a sweet girl, but she gets a little too headstrong about things."

"Things like lighthouses?"

"Well, yes," Patty agreed. "Are you hoping I'll have insight about Mitchell Collins' murder? I don't think Skye did it, for what my word is worth."

"I don't think she did either," Genny acknowledged. "But I'm helping the police and I need to follow every lead. She's been using your paint in her protests."

"Ah," Patty said, readjusting her seating position with a groan. "Has she?"

"You must have known that," Genny said. If Patty had been watching the social media videos, she would surely have seen the bottle of paint in Skye's hand.

"Perhaps, perhaps not," Patty answered vaguely. "What's the connection between my paint and the murder?"

"Skye threw your paint over the lighthouse whilst protesting its construction. And Mitchell Collins was found with that same paint splattered across him."

"So, whoever did it bought my paint, perhaps to frame Skye," Patty concluded. "Would it be helpful for you to see my ledgers? I keep a record of every customer."

"That… that would be very helpful, actually," Genny said. She admired how forthcoming the older woman was.

"It's no problem," Patty said with a small shrug, putting down her mug of tea and heaving herself to her feet with a groan.

They headed back to the counter and Patty flipped through the ledger.

"How many bottles do you think they used?" She asked. "Plenty of people buy just one or two, usually for their kids' school projects."

"We're looking for someone who bought at least ten bottles," Genny said, estimating based on the amount of paint at the crime scene.

"There are a few people who buy that colour in bulk," Patty answered, running her finger down the page. "Are you ready to take notes?"

"Yes." She pulled her phone from her pocket and opened the notes app.

"Last month, Skye – I'm sure you could guess that one. She bought twenty bottles."

"You didn't question that?"

"She's arty," Patty shrugged, although the slight grin at the edge of her mouth suggested to Genny that maybe she was more clued up on the nature of the protests than she was pretending to be. "Then, a couple of weeks later, a schoolteacher called Darren? No, Derek. Derek Canterbury bought fifteen bottles. Sorry, I can barely read my own handwriting."

"That's okay, keep going," Genny encouraged.

"Then, a few weeks ago a local artist called Vanessa… What does that say? Well, Vanessa something or other bought twelve bottles. Two weeks ago, Jean Hillier who runs the nursery bought ten bottles. And about ten days ago… Will? Bill? Smith? Smint?"

"It looks like 'Stent'," Genny suggested.

"Could be," Patty agreed. "I remember him. Older guy, dark hair which was turning grey. Very quiet. It says here that he bought fifteen bottles."

"Anyone else?" Genny said, hoping a name would stick out. None of the people she had listed so far were on the suspects list.

"Not since the summer," Patty said, scrolling back through. "The community centre bought fifty bottles of assorted colours for their youth group to paint a mural in June. I helped out with it myself."

"Okay," she sighed. "Thank you for your time. I have no idea if this will lead anywhere, but it could all be important for finding the killer."

"You are welcome here anytime," Patty said warmly. "For anything."

8

Genny and Pearl walked up to the police station, situated in a modern building on the edge of town.

She tried to distract herself as they waited for Remy, her eyes flitting from the uniformed officers to the military grey walls uncomfortably.

"This is all just a formality, Genny," Superintendent Soon-Yi had told her in the waiting room of the police station nearest to Genny's house. "You know I have to ask you some questions about your sister's death, but it doesn't mean you are suspected of anything, and you still have all of your rights, including the right to legal representation if you would like it."

Genny hadn't been able to reply, looking down at her hands, shaking in front of her.

"Genny?" Remy broke the reverie as he came out from the door behind the reception. "Is everything okay?"

"This is my neighbour," Genny explained. "Pearl has some evidence to submit for the case."

"Yes," Pearl said quickly, keen not to get into trouble. "It's about Mitchell's wife."

"Okay," Remy said. "Go through and the officer will help you fill in some forms."

"Thank you," Pearl said, looking sheepishly at Genny.

"What was that all about?" Remy asked Genny as he followed her out to the car park.

She could breathe easier, letting out the breath she hadn't known she was holding.

"Nosey neighbour, nothing to worry about," Genny explained. "The video evidence she showed me is of Yolanda Collins and Mitchell's friend Paul, kissing in the street outside my new house."

"They were having an affair?"

"It seems so. According to Pearl, Yolanda was with Mitchell for his money. Perhaps we were looking at the wrong family member. Jake certainly didn't seem fond of his stepmother."

"Maybe it's time we called on Yolanda again," Remy said.

"Are you here to see Jake, Inspector?" Yolanda asked as she opened the door to them.

Genny marked how different she looked – the casual clothes from just a few days earlier were replaced by a tight red dress, her blonde hair pinned up on the back of her head.

"No, actually, we need to speak to you again, Mrs. Collins," Remy said. He gestured to her outfit. "Are you on your way out?"

"No," she said, the lie obvious from her pink cheeks. "I just thought it was time to start getting back to normal."

She moved aside to let them in.

"We won't sit down, if that's okay," Remy said, his tone a little firmer than usual. "We just have a few questions."

"Okay…" Yolanda shrugged, rounding the kitchen island.

Genny remembered the technique – don't let anyone get too settled or comfortable. She could often extract far more from the witness that way.

"I'll cut to the chase," Remy said, crossing his arms. "We know you were having an affair with your husband's best friend, Paul Steventon."

Genny tried not to let her surprise show on her face. They didn't know that detail for a fact – all they knew was that they had shared a kiss. But the assumption would put her on the backfoot if true.

"Oh," Yolanda said, turning her back to them as she reached into the cupboard above the sink and pulled out a tray of glasses and a bottle of whiskey. She decanted a double into one glass and gestured to them both.

"No, thank you," Genny said, speaking for them both. "Do you deny that you were having an affair with Mr. Steventon?"

"Ha," Yolanda said, downing the drink. "I thought it was common knowledge by now."

"Why was that?" Genny asked.

"That snake of an ex-wife – Loretta. She was always looking for dirt on me, and she got the perfect ammunition when she walked in on me and Paul in my bedroom. I was certain she would tell Mitchell, quickly followed by the whole island."

"And she didn't?"

"It seems not," Yolanda smiled manically, pouring another drink. "She's craftier than I thought."

"How long ago did Loretta discover that you were cheating on your husband?" Remy asked.

"About two months ago," Yolanda sighed and then paused. "Is that not how you found out about us?"

"No," Remy said. "We had... other sources. You were seen together."

"Hmm," Yolanda chuckled. "I guess we weren't as careful as I thought we were." She downed another drink and took another moment to formulate her thoughts. "I see why you're here. You think this gives me a motive to kill my husband."

"Can you deny that having Mitchell out of the way wouldn't have made things easier?" Remy asked tersely. He was pushing, carefully leaning on her to get the truth.

"You are presuming that I wanted to be with Paul," Yolanda shrugged.

"Is that not why you are all dressed up?" Genny suggested. "Or do you often sit at home drinking in a £400 designer dress?"

Remy's mouth curled slightly, trying to hide a smirk.

"Fine," Yolanda admitted. "I was going to join him for lunch after his cycling meet this morning. But that doesn't mean that I wanted to be with him. He's always just been… fun. Mitchell was more than that."

She looked down tearfully.

"And what about Paul?" Remy leaned on the kitchen island, keeping eye contact with her. "Is it just casual for him? Or might he have wanted your husband out of the picture too?"

"That's ridiculous," Yolanda shook her head derisively. "Paul's not a murderer…"

But although her words were firm, her eyes drifted away from Remy's, unsure and questioning it herself.

"Okay, I think we have everything we need," Remy said, turning back towards the door.

"Wait!" Yolanda said. "He loves me, he wouldn't kill Mitchell."

"The fact that he loves you, might be just the reason that he would kill Mitchell," Remy asserted. "We might be in touch again. Have a good day, Mrs. Collins."

The Westmarsh Cycling Club was a sports centre on the edge of the wetlands, with easy access to the coastal paths and the quiet roads of the village itself.

Remy and Genny narrowly avoided being slammed into their car as they walked out across the car park, a large group of road-bikers zooming back towards the side entrance.

"Watch it!" One of them shouted.

"Oh, I hate cyclists," Remy murmured. "The Lycra gives me P.E flashbacks."

"They're worse in London," Genny grinned, enjoying the uncharacteristic look of disdain on his face. "Aerodynamic peaches in every direction."

"Oh, what a horrible image," Remy shuddered. "Is it an attractive look?"

"I think there's something to be said for a Chris Froome type."

"Even with the big thighs?"

"That's the main appeal, I think," Genny chuckled.

Remy grimaced again and she laughed.

The receptionist took them through to the bike shed, where the group from the cycling meet were talking, just having finished. The room was clean and modern, but with the dank smell of old sweat still pervading it.

"Paul Steventon?" Remy asked, flashing his police badge as the group ignored him and continued with the conversation. "Mr. Steventon?"

Paul turned to them, still laughing from the conversation, his face falling as he noticed the badge. He took off his helmet and hung it from the handlebars of his bike.

"Yes? What do you want?" He asked, walking towards the changing rooms.

Remy and Genny followed, keeping up the pace as Paul snaked through the changing room towards his locker.

"We need to speak to you about the murder of Mitchell Collins," Remy said. "We've just been to see his widow, Yolanda."

"Ah," Paul said, opening his locker and starting to undress, sweeping off the first piece of Lycra in one swift motion. Remy shot a look at Genny who held back a laugh. They turned away as he continued, "Mitchell was my closest friend, but I'm sure you know that already."

"We do," Genny nodded, still averting her gaze as he unabashedly pulled off his leggings. "We also know that you were having an affair with Yolanda Collins."

Paul faced them, now shirtless, his eyes wide in surprise.

"How... how do you know that? Did Yolanda tell you that?" He stuttered.

"She all but admitted it. She also told us that you were caught by Loretta Collins," Remy explained.

Paul scrunched up the t-shirt in his hand and sank onto the bench in the centre of the changing room.

"God, what a mess," he groaned. "What must you think of me now? You might not believe me when I say this, but Mitchell was my best mate. I've never had a friend like him. I would have done anything for him, and I certainly wouldn't have killed him, if that's what you're here to imply."

"You would have done anything for him, except stop seeing his wife?" Genny scoffed. "Forgive us if we don't quite see the logic there."

"It was complicated," Paul shrugged. "Haven't you ever been in love with someone you shouldn't have been in love with?"

"Not at the expense of my so-called best friend," Remy snapped back. "So, you should tell us quickly where you were at the time of the murder."

"I... I was here, I think," Mitchell said. "I remember Yolanda coming to find me after she identified his body. She was in pieces, as you can imagine. I had just finished a cycle. I was probably out on the bike while it was happening. We're all training for the competition this weekend."

"Can anyone corroborate that?" Remy asked.

"A few of the guys from the club were with me," Paul said. "We must have taken the route up to the wetlands and then down alongside the river towards Waldemere Lake."

"I was with him," a man piped up from behind them. "We were out from 4pm to about 6.30pm and then we got a coffee in the clubhouse."

Remy blew out his breath as he looked at Genny. It was as watertight an alibi as they could hope for.

"Right," Remy nodded. "We'll need your name and contact details, plus anyone else who can vouch for Paul's whereabouts."

"Certainly," the man nodded. "Speak to Laura at reception, she signed us in, plus Deb and Ahmed who work at the clubhouse served us."

"Thank you for your time," Genny said. "I'm sure we'll be back if we need to ask you anything else."

"Before you go," Paul said quickly. "This is all confidential, isn't it? I don't want anyone to find out me and Yolanda are... whatever we are now."

"Of course," Genny said, resisting the urge to tell him what she really thought of him.

Poor Mitchell had been surrounded by liars, cheaters and backstabbers. And yet, there was still nothing that lined up with a clear-cut motive for his murder.

9

Remy bought them both lunch in *The Water's Edge* as they reviewed the case notes again, desperate to see a pattern emerge somewhere. Genny filled him in on her trip to Patty's shop and everything she had found out about the paint.

"It's the most illogical case I've ever seen," Remy sighed, keeping his voice quiet as the pub bustled with other patrons. He took a bite of his sandwich and paused in thought. "There are plenty of people with opportunity – a remote location, out of view of anyone, even the crowd gathered around the other side – and acquiring a gun is easy enough for someone determined to pull this off, as it seems our killer was. But it's the motive. Who could actually hate Mitchell Collins enough to plan and execute his murder?"

"I can't make sense of it either," Genny said, biting her lip as she looked over the notes again. "I was so certain that his money had to play a role, but both Yolanda and Jake don't seem to have a motive."

"And they both have watertight alibis, as it turns out," Remy said, pointing to a page in his notebook. "Yolanda and Loretta were having dinner together with a couple of neighbours – can you imagine how awkward that grouping must have been? And Jake was seen leaving your house after the events at the lighthouse – Pearl's security footage turned out to be doubly useful after all."

"Perhaps I should have let her keep it installed," Genny grinned.

"Only if you remember to keep your curtains pulled," Remy laughed.

"So, everything is a dead end," Genny summarised. "And in my experience, that is a lead in itself."

"How do you mean?"

"Well, to para-phrase Sherlock Holmes – if you remove everything impossible, whatever left, however improbable, must be true. Perhaps the truth of this case is that the motive is improbable."

"How do we find a motive if it is improbable?"

"By looking at the centre of this case, the thing everything leads back to – the lighthouse itself," Genny suggested. "What if the motive for this murder had nothing to do with Mitchell? What if he was a statement, like we suggested before?"

"I thought we ruled out Skye Devon and the protestors?" Remy shrugged.

"Maybe someone else wanted the lighthouse re-opening to fail," Genny offered. "What about Roisin? She seems to be the long-suffering daughter of a corporate moron. Could she have snapped under the pressure?"

"It's a possibility," Remy agreed.

"Or perhaps the reason goes back further than the Nobels." Genny leaned back in her chair and thought through everything she had learnt about the lighthouse and the history of the island. "My neighbour, Pearl, said the lighthouse had a dark history – lots of deaths in the 1800s."

"Do you think a ghost from the 1800s came back to kill Mitchell?" Remy teased.

"That might fall into the 'impossible' category," Genny smiled. "But what if someone wants to make the lighthouse look... cursed?"

"We should look up its history in the island's archives in Gentleweir," Remy offered, taking a large bite of his sandwich and dusting off his hands. "Let's head up there now."

Genny concurred, gathering up her things.

Just as Remy was putting on his coat, his phone rang.

"Hello?" He answered, his face falling instantly. "Okay. Okay – I'll be there shortly." He hung up and turned to Genny, "The archives will have to wait – there's been an attack at the lighthouse."

10

Remy's car screeched on the unmade track as they flew up towards the lighthouse, the blue lights of several other police cars clear on the horizon.

They jumped out of the car to find Roisin Nobel wrapped in a foil blanket on a bench to the rear of the building, the crime scene still just as it had been left. A man around her age was stood just behind her, a comforting hand on her shoulder.

"Miss Nobel," Remy said as they approached. "Please tell us what happened."

She was shaking, but she cleared her throat and steadied herself as she took care to answer slowly, "I had a phone call from a potential client, wanting Dad to work with them to renovate and redesign an old warehouse they had bought in Owlwood. They had heard about his other projects around the island

and were impressed." She took another deep, shuddering breath.

"Just take your time," Genny said gently, crouching down at her level.

"They wanted to meet at the lighthouse," Roisin explained. "Which I thought was a little strange, given what happened here, but they said they wanted to see my dad's work up close."

"They specifically mentioned the lighthouse?" Remy asked, sharing a look with Genny.

That was suspicious in itself.

Why would someone insist on meeting at the scene of a murder?

"Yes," Roisin answered with a sharp nod. "They were insistent that it had to be here, and that I should come alone. Dad was busy, so I didn't know what to do at first. He'd be so upset with me for turning away potential business, especially after the re-opening went so... well, after what happened to Mitchell."

So, Kristian had been released, probably with no more than a slap on the wrist for his aggressive behaviour.

But that begged the question, why Roisin? If the client wanted to see Kristian's work, why not ask the man himself to show you?

None of it added up.

"I see," Remy said. "Then what happened?"

"My boyfriend, Sam," she gestured to the man behind her, gripping his hand on her shoulder for support. "Thought it was a bit weird, so he said he would drive me and wait in the car. Then…" She paused again, sobs threatening to take her over until she swallowed them down again. "Then I felt this whack on the back of my head. I lost consciousness, and when I woke up, Sam told me what happened."

Remy turned his attention to Sam.

"I was scrolling through my InstaPost feed in the car, then I heard a yelp. I looked up and there was a person over Roisin, she was on the ground, her head bleeding. They looked like they were about to hit her again, so I just ran out of the car, shouting. They turned and ran down the cliff path, and I ran over to Roisin to see if she was okay."

"Thank goodness you were here," Roisin sobbed, gripping Sam's hand again.

"Could you describe the person, Sam?" Genny asked. "Would you know them if you saw them again?"

"No," Sam shrugged. "They were prepared. Dressed all in black, with a big, long black raincoat. It went all the way down to their shins and they had the hood up."

"Could you try to tell us what their body type was? Could you see their hair or skin colour?" Genny pushed.

"I couldn't see any hair or skin…" he thought, closing his eyes to picture the scene. "They were medium height or tall-ish, maybe 5'11 and slim. They ran really fast when they heard me."

"What did they hit Roisin with? Did you see a weapon?" Remy said, pulling his notebook from his pocket and writing out Sam's answers.

"It looked like a statue," Sam shrugged. "Big, and heavy."

"Metal?"

"Stone, I think. Marbled. They took it when they ran."

Not the sort of thing someone grabs when they plan a murder, Genny thought. If this was the same person that killed Mitchell, the motive was different this time, more desperate, erratic.

"Okay, thank you," Genny said. "If you remember anything else about them, it's really important that you tell us."

"We're going to put police protection on you, Roisin," Remy said. "The killer may try again."

"Really?" Roisin asked, the terror clear on her face. "Why are they trying to kill me? Is it the same person who killed Mitchell?"

"We're not sure yet," Genny said. "It seems that way, but we can't be sure at this stage in the investigation."

"You're telling me I'm in danger and you don't know why?" Roisin said, giving into the tears and breaking down, Sam wrapping an arm around her.

"We're going to keep you safe," Remy assured her. "The ambulance will be here shortly, and you will have a police presence wherever you are until we catch this killer."

Roisin nodded tearfully, clinging to Sam's arm.

"Are you sure there's nothing else you can tell us?" Genny asked, watching Roisin's distraught face carefully. "It seems likely that this attack is related to the murder of Mitchell Collins. Anything you might know about his murder might help us work out who is after you."

Roisin looked down.

She knew something.

Just as Genny had suspected. The killer had targeted her for a reason.

"I didn't know if it was relevant," Roisin sniffled.

"Anything you can tell us, no matter how small, could be a big clue," Genny assured her, taking her hands in hers.

"I saw…" Roisin murmured. "I didn't know what I saw, until today. I saw someone in a big black raincoat at the lighthouse, just before Dad arrived to start the opening. I was the only person up here and they seemed to turn and walk away quite fast when they saw me. At the time I presumed they were just a walker, because of how they were dressed. I didn't see their face or any features. But after Sam described my attacker, I knew it was the same person."

"Thank you, Roisin, that's really useful," Genny said, squeezing her hands a final time and turning to Remy.

They walked back to the car, both deep in thought.

"This has to be our killer," Remy said.

"I was thinking the same thing," Genny agreed. "Roisin's sighting of them before the opening must have made them worry that she could ID the killer to us. Her phone is always ringing, I expect they took the first opportunity to make a fake appointment that they could."

"We need to keep a watch on Roisin," Remy said. "And once her injuries have been seen to, we might have to use her to lure out the killer."

11

Genny felt torn about asking Roisin to put herself in harm's way again, but she had agreed with Remy that it was the best way to bring the killer out into the open. Without this attack, they had little to go on.

Thankfully, Roisin agreed to be used as bait for the killer, and Genny knew of just the event for it.

The Westmarsh Cycling Club were holding a competition that weekend, a race around the coastal paths, past the now infamous lighthouse and back down towards Westmarsh.

Remy had arranged for plain clothes police officers to watch out for Roisin, with Genny and Remy nearby too, making it look like she was alone, watching the race from the bench by the lighthouse. On the morning of the race, they had her post a selfie on the bench, with the caption 'Day out with me, myself and I while the boyfriend is playing football. Excited to watch the #WestmarshCycle40K from a quiet spot by this cute little lighthouse owned by my Dad @kristiannobelbusiness'.

The bait was set, and although Genny knew that there were plenty of people nearby to watch out for Roisin, she was nervous.

Her and Remy sat further down the coastal path, hidden behind a grass hillock, sipping tea from a flask.

"I'm betting it's been a while since you did something like this," Remy said.

"A long time," Genny agreed. "Although sting operations in London were usually a lot less picturesque and involved a dark alleyway full of drug needles."

"I'd rather be here than there for sure," Remy smiled, looking down at the beach below the cliffs. "But what made you give it up? You clearly didn't retire because of old age. And you must have enjoyed your work?"

"It's… a long story," Genny sighed. She wanted to tell him all about Annabelle, but the words just wouldn't come out no matter how many times she thought about it. She didn't want his eyes to fill with pity, his words to soften. That was what happened every time she told someone what had happened to her sister and the events after.

"Sorry, I won't push you," Remy said. "It's none of my business."

"No, I... I just don't know where to start," Genny stalled, desperate to find the words to tell him. "My sister..."

She cut herself off as Remy looked through the binoculars and tapped her arm.

"There!" He said, pulling his radio from his pocket as he handed her the binoculars. "Eight-four, we have a sighting, can you confirm? Over."

"Roger that. Over," the voice on the other end answered.

Genny peered through the binoculars.

A woman in a black raincoat was making her way up the coastal path towards the lighthouse, walking fast as she noticed Roisin.

"Eight-four we're making our way towards you. Over," Remy said as Genny dropped the flask and they started at a run up the path, a few officers appearing nearer to the scene and stopping the woman in her tracks.

They reached the lighthouse, Roisin looking equal parts terrified and confused as the plain clothes officers argued with the woman. She was in her mid-60s with greying brown hair.

"Let me pass!" She squeaked, her hands on her hips. "Who are you?"

"I'm DI Remy Cochran," Remy answered, pulling his badge. "Could you please tell us your name and why you are here?"

The woman crossed her arms indignantly.

"And what is it exactly that you're accusing me of doing? Walking?" She snapped. "I'm just taking my dog out, as I often have done for the past decade."

She gestured to a Jack Russell who was weeing against a rock a few hundred metres ahead of the woman.

"Even so, we need your name," Remy insisted. "This is important police business. A murder was committed here last week."

"Oh," the woman said, her cheeks growing whiter. "I did hear, it's awfully sad."

"Your name," Genny pressed.

"Vanessa Wollstonecraft," she answered. "I'll co-operate however you need me to, officers."

"We need to know where you were on the 5th between 4 and 6pm," Genny said.

"On the 5th?" Vanessa repeated back, thinking. "That was a Saturday, wasn't it? I think I was with my mother, Alma Berry, in Gentleweir."

"I see," Remy said. "We will need to take you and your mother's contact details and address."

"Of course," Vanessa said with a shrug. "But I still don't understand - what did I do wrong?"

"Maybe nothing at all," Remy sighed.

Genny deflated as she looked the woman up and down. She certainly didn't seem like their killer, calculating and merciless. She looked genuinely shocked by their appearance.

They headed back down the hill as Remy phoned Vanessa's elderly mother, who confirmed that she had been with her until 8pm, when she had returned home.

"It was one heck of a coincidence," Remy said. "She really did match the description Sam and Roisin gave."

"We will try again," Genny said. "The murderer isn't going to give up on Roisin so easily if they think she can identify them."

"It's a shame that Roisin didn't actually see their face, or at the very least give us a skin colour or hair colour. I still feeling like we're searching in the dark."

"Not completely in the dark," Genny reminded him.

"The archives," Remy nodded, remembering their previous plan. "Perhaps we'll finally find what we're looking for. I have a feeling that you're right – this has more to do with the lighthouse than Mitchell Collins."

12

Gentleweir was a small town a short drive from Whitebourne on the northern coast of the island, and just as picturesque. The town was famous for its canal, which stretched from the eastern side all the way to Market Yaxley, and was popular with pleasure boaters, canoers and houseboats alike.

The riverbanks were populated with moored houseboats and the town had grown an economy around them, with cafes, a farm shop and boat supply shop dotted along the riverbank.

The newspaper archives were in the library in the centre of the town, an old 18th century mill which now housed the island's largest collection of antique books and boasted a climate-controlled cellar for particularly old editions.

"The archives have compiled all newspaper articles from the past one hundred and eleven years," the archivist, a chirpy middle-aged lady called Helena told them as she led them through the library to a large room upstairs. The air felt heavy with dust, and the small windows (original to the 18th century structure) let in only a small amount of light.

"It isn't digitalised?" Genny asked. Remy turned away his face to hide a look that said, 'this isn't London'.

"No," Helena tittered, amused at the idea. "We're a small trust, funded by donations to the Solent Island Preservation Society. We can't afford fancy equipment or to pay someone for their time putting it all into a computer. It would take months. But for now, everything is laid out by location and then by year."

"So, Sandhaven Lighthouse would be…" Remy looked around the room until he spotted the shelves labelled 'Sandhaven'.

"Exactly," Helena said, locating the exact shelf. "This one is all about the lighthouse."

"Thank you so much for your help," Genny smiled, feeling a little daunted by the out-of-date catalogue. She had been used to computer systems filing articles, documents and evidence by minute details, easily searchable. This would be a learning curve.

Helena left them with the boxes and returned downstairs.

"Only five boxes," Remy commented.

"A little surprising, given its long history," Genny said. "I suppose a lighthouse is rarely newsworthy."

Most entries were very old, mentioning its renovations and various lighthouse keepers during the late 19th century and early 20th century.

"Here," Genny said, pulling an article from thirty years ago. "This piece was written when a new light was put in. It says that the lighthouse used to be manually operated. The light had to be turned on and off by the lighthouse keeper, as well as maintained and checked to make sure it was functioning correctly."

Remy leaned over to read the article with her.

"Wow," he whistled through his teeth. "It cost £10,000 – that's more than £30,000 in today's money."

"It was funded by the Solent Island Preservation Society," Genny said, pointing to another line in the article. "They held a dance competition to help raise the money."

"That's how important it was," Remy nodded. "The lighthouse is all but decorative now, but back then it saved lives."

"I wonder what the Solent Island Preservation Society thought of the lighthouse closing down twenty years ago, given how important it seemed to be."

"I don't remember why exactly it closed," Remy commented, blinking in thought. "I know the official line is that the last lighthouse keeper retired, and no one took his place."

"I wonder if that was the whole story," Genny said pointedly.

They rifled through the second box, finding photos and more articles about restoration to the lighthouse.

"Look at this," Remy said, pulling an article from the third box. "This is from twenty years ago, just before the lighthouse closed."

They placed the article on the table and pulled a lamp closer, looking over it together:

Boat accident kills four passengers.

"This is what my neighbour was talking about," Genny said. "She mentioned some sort of accident."

A boat crashed into the rocks below Sandhaven clifftop on Friday evening when a private group took a hired boat out into the bay. Officials have determined the primary cause of the accident was the rough seas, but locals are laying blame at the door of Sandy Wirral (43) the keeper of Sandhaven Lighthouse.

"43?" Remy interrupted. "Hardly retirement age."

"No, not even close to retirement age," Genny agreed, tracing her finger along and continuing:

Eyewitness reports claim that the lighthouse's beam was not shining its warning out into the sea that evening, with some claiming that the four deaths are the result of Mr. Wirral's negligence.

This is not the first time that Mr. Wirral has come under fire from the community. In 1989, a fishing boat snagged on the rocks, claiming that the lighthouse was flickering rather than offering a steady beam. While nobody was killed in that incident, the deaths of the four Gentleweir residents are being laid firmly at Mr. Wirral's door.

"Do you remember this?" Genny asked. "It was twenty years ago, but it must have been a shock to the community."

"Now that I've read that… I think so," Remy nodded pensively. "I was in school, fourteen or so. I think we had someone from the RNLI come into class to talk about being safe on the water after that."

"Who were the victims?" Genny asked. "The article doesn't say."

"No, it doesn't," Remy said, pulling his tablet from his bag. "Let's see if there's an address for Sandy Wirral."

He logged into the police database and only one result came up.

"12 Coalbag Lane, Gentleweir," Genny read from the screen. "This is where he lived after the lighthouse closed – do you think he would still be there? He'd only be in his early to mid-60s now?"

"Let's find out," Remy said.

The cottage on Coalbag Lane was clearly empty from the outside, with no curtains or blinds to obscure the unfurnished and unlived in rooms.

Remy knocked a few times, but there was no answer.

"Damn it," Genny groaned. "How can this be a dead end? Everything pointed to the mystery of why the lighthouse closed twenty years ago."

"Hello?" A quiet voice called to them.

A woman was standing in the front garden of the cottage next door. She was eighty or older, dressed in a long polka dot dress and leather shoes.

"Hello," Genny said. She smiled back.

"Can I help you?" The lady asked.

"We're with the police," Remy explained, showing his badge. "We're looking for Sandy Wirral – he used to live here."

"Oh," the lady nodded knowingly. "Yes, I remember him. He abandoned the cottage some years ago."

"Can you remember how long ago that was?" Genny asked.

"Not long after he moved in," the lady pondered. "Twenty or so years ago."

"Do you know where he went?" Remy questioned. "Did he leave you with a forwarding address?"

The lady scoffed, "Oh, I know where he went, that coward." She shook her head disapprovingly. "He ran away, went to live with his mother on the mainland. He rented out the house for a while, but the last tenants moved out over a year ago."

"He went to England?" Remy confirmed.

"Yes," the lady said, pulling her cardigan tighter around her. "But he came back last week. I saw him in Whitebourne and I thought I'd seen a ghost!"

"He's in Whitebourne?" Genny asked quickly, her pulse rising.

This was it – he had to have come back for the lighthouse re-opening.

But where was he now? Could he somehow be Mitchell's murderer?

"He told me he's staying at *The Mudlark*," the lady shrugged. "But he didn't want anyone else to know he was here. Kept his hood up. I expect he's ashamed, and so he should be."

Ashamed about the accident, or ashamed about murdering an innocent man?

But what possible motive could the old lighthouse keeper have to murder Mitchell Collins?

"The other guest at the *The Mudlark*," Genny said to Remy. "Bev and Tom said that he doesn't come downstairs. That must be Sandy."

"I'm going in now – it's far too nippy out here," the lady said. "I hope you find that ratbag of a man. He should pay for what he did."

The lady shuffled back inside her house, muttering under her breath about shirked responsibilities and cowardly men as she did.

"We should head back to Whitebourne, and quickly," Remy said, leading Genny back towards the car. "If he was only here for the lighthouse re-opening, I doubt he'll be staying much longer."

13

"Genny, you're back just in time for afternoon tea!" Bev twittered as they approached the front steps of *The Mudlark*. She was knelt by the flowerbeds out the front, planting tulip bulbs in a neat row. Pip – the Beechams having eagerly agreed to watch her while Genny was busy - was rolling in the grass next to her and Genny leaned down to rub the dog's belly.

"I'm sorry, Bev, we're here on police business," Genny said, her heart sinking as she saw the look of shock on Bev's face. She hastily added, "We need to speak to your other guest – the man you mentioned."

"Oh," Bev said, groaning as she pushed herself up from her knees. Remy took her hand to help her up. "I think he's in his room, but you should hurry – he said he wanted to check out this evening."

"Thank you, Bev," Remy said, with an affectionate squeeze of the older lady's hand. "We'll keep the disruption to a minimum."

They made their way up the stairs and knocked on the door for Room 3.

At first it seemed as if he had already gone. Genny anxiously tapped her fingers against her thigh as they waited, but eventually they heard the sound of the chain being removed and the door opened by a few inches.

"Yes?" The man said, reluctantly peering through the crack in the door.

"Sandy Wirral?" Remy asked. "I'm Detective Inspector Remy Cochran with the Solent Island police. We need to speak to you."

"Oh," the man said, opening the door fully, his lips pursed tensely. "Yes, I'm Sandy."

He was in his mid-60s just as they had guessed, with dark hair, dotted with grey patches. He was dishevelled, the look of someone who was grappling with themselves, in old, worn jeans and a fleece jacket. His jacket was red with green squares on it, just as worn as his other items of clothing.

A shudder ran up Genny.

This was the man she had seen at the lighthouse opening, skulking away as the Nobels made their speeches.

"We need to speak to you about the murder of Mitchell Collins," Remy said matter-of-factly.

Sandy's face collapsed as he tried to close the door on them, Genny shoving her left foot in the way quickly.

"I didn't have anything to do with that! Leave me alone!" Sandy barked, still trying to close the door.

His expression was contorted with distress, but not guilt or anger. He looked scared, vulnerable, and desperate.

"Sandy – it's okay," Genny said gently. She couldn't be certain that he was innocent, but the look on his face seemed hard to fake. She was determined to say anything to keep the conversation going. "We know you didn't kill him."

She really hoped that was the truth. He seemed too sweet to be a killer.

Sandy stopped trying to close the door, meeting Genny's gaze, panting hard and tears welling in his eyes.

"I shouldn't have gone up there," Sandy said. "I should have just stayed away, that's what everyone wanted me to do."

"Who?" Remy asked.

"The whole island!" Sandy said, a tear breaking free and rolling down his cheek. "Everyone who blamed me for the accident twenty years ago!"

"That's why you left," Genny nodded. "Because everyone blamed you."

"And because I blame myself!" Sandy said shakily, his knuckles going red from their grip on the door handle. "How could I not? If I hadn't gone out that night, if I had checked the light more thoroughly… it was my fault that the light didn't shine that night."

"That sounds like an accident," Genny said.

"I went out. I was desperate to be defined by something other than my job. You know, I was in that lighthouse all day, every day. I didn't have friends. I barely saw my family. Then, I met someone, and I hoped I could maybe have a future with them…"

"And the light malfunctioned while you were out," Genny guessed.

"Yes. I thought I would be back in time for the sun going down, but I was having fun. I got back only an hour after sunset, but it was too late. The light hadn't turned on and that boat… that boat had crashed." He choked as sobs rose up in his throat. "I could see the emergency services in the water below the cliffs, five or six boats trying to help those poor people…"

"Sandy, you didn't cause their deaths," she said gently. "They went out in rough seas at sunset, even if they hadn't hit the rocks, they were being reckless. It was an accident."

"An accident that will always be linked to my negligence!" Sandy spat. "The whole village saw me out that evening, having dinner with someone who never wanted to see me again after that. Everyone blamed me. Including her."

"That was unfair of them," Remy said. "You made a mistake."

"Now you see why I had to leave," Sandy said. "The community I had grown up in became a mob, hellbent on chasing me out."

"So, why did you come back?" Genny asked. "To see the lighthouse?"

"Yes," Sandy nodded. "I live on the mainland now, taking care of my elderly mother. We saw on article online when Kristian Nobel bought the lighthouse. It said he was renovating it in order to reopen it. I felt I had to come and see it."

"But you left," Genny said. "I saw you."

"Someone recognised me," Sandy said. "A woman who had worked at the bakery in Whitebourne back then. I thought I better leave before the witch hunt started again."

"But you stayed in Whitebourne? Why?" Remy pressed.

"After I heard that poor man had been murdered, I couldn't face going home thinking that history was repeating itself. More tragedy because of that stupid lighthouse!"

Footsteps coming up the stairs made all three of them turn – it was Tom.

"I'm sorry to interrupt, Inspector, but Mr. Wirral's taxi is here," Tom said.

Sandy grabbed his suitcase from behind him and tried to move past them.

"Wait!" Genny said. "You're leaving?"

"I've stayed here long enough," Sandy answered. "My mother needs me."

Genny and Remy followed him down to the taxi.

"You're really going to leave again? You're going to let the mob destroy you?"

"No one wants me here," Sandy said. "Just please find that poor man's killer."

And with that, he ducked into the taxi.

"He's a tortured soul," Genny said. "One mistake and he was blamed for the death of four people."

"He looked completely haunted by it," Remy concurred. "Those clothes looked twenty years old if not more. He's punishing himself more than the people of Whitebourne ever could."

"His clothes…" Genny exclaimed, locking eyes with Remy and thinking fast. "That's it!"

"What?" Remy asked, trying to follow her train of thought.

The image of Mitchell Collins at Foxglove Cottage the day of his murder came to her mind.

Dust-coated worn jeans. A red and green tartan jacket.

Salt and pepper hair.

"We have been looking in the wrong place all along," Genny burst out. "Nothing made sense because we were trying to work out why someone would want to kill *Mitchell*."

"Well, yes…" Remy said, still not following.

"Think about it – Sandy and Mitchell. In the setting sun, from behind, in similar clothes…"

"They'd look very alike," Remy agreed, picking up her idea. "You think that the killer mistook one for the other?"

The theory gathered pace in Genny's head.

"Where's your tablet?" Genny said hurriedly, Remy producing it from his bag.

They stared at the screen as she searched for 'Sandhaven Lighthouse accident'.

"We looked through the archives," Remy reminded her as they scrolled.

"The archives weren't digitalised," she reminded him. "They only included physical newspaper reports."

"You think there will be a more recent online report?"

"Here!" She said triumphantly, handing the tablet back to him and pointing at the title. "A follow-up article marking twenty years since the accident."

He skimmed the text and then quoted from it, "'The victims were 50-year-old Gentleweir residents Trent Brooke and his wife Felicity, her sister Kira and her godson… 19-year-old Logan Wollstonecraft."

"Wollstonecraft!" Genny said. "There can't be many people on the island with that name. I knew this had to do with the lighthouse… it's too much of a coincidence."

"I agree. Vanessa was bluffing," Remy said. He shook with head incredulous and ran his hands up and down his face. "If he was 19 then... he could have been her son."

"It's a motive. Her son was killed in the accident. She blamed Sandy," Genny rattled off, starting to stride the pavement in thought. "But there was no justice to be served because it wasn't solely his fault. The Brookes shouldn't have taken the boat out in those conditions, lighthouse or no lighthouse."

"And with them dead, Vanessa had no one left to blame but Sandy," Remy said, following her logic.

"But why wait until now to try to kill him?"

"He was on the mainland, perhaps she didn't know how to find him," Remy suggested.

"But now he's here... and so is she."

"I'll call the station to get pick up Sandy. In the meantime, we need to get Vanessa."

"You're right," Genny said. "We can't risk her staying free."

"We have her number, but she's hardly likely to agree to meet us."

"No, but she might agree to meet Roisin," Genny said. "I'll call Roisin, you organise the officers."

Vanessa was waiting for Roisin by the lighthouse when Remy and Genny pulled up, tapping her hands together with impatient irritation. Vanessa's dog sat at her side, looking up at her.

Her eyes widened when she saw them, her face falling in horror as Sandy stepped out of the car too.

Without hesitation, she started to sprint down the cliff path, her dog looking around, confused.

Genny and Remy gave chase, scrambling on the loose stones. Genny tried not to focus on the height, keeping up the pace as Vanessa wound her way down towards the beach.

After a few minutes, the steep path joined onto the sand, and Vanessa ran across it, leaving deep boot prints. Genny could hear sirens somewhere on the roads around them, the police desperately trying to find a way down to them.

Remy was faster than her, long legs skimming along the top of the sand with ease, but Genny started to fall off, Pip jumping up at her side as she sensed her distress.

"Pip, help," Genny said breathlessly. She pointed towards Vanessa, and the spaniel cocked her head knowingly before taking off at full speed across the beach.

Pip bounded towards Vanessa, who was starting to struggle too, stumbling as the wet sand grew deeper.

Pip caught up to her, barking at her heels and causing Vanessa to cry out, turning sharply across towards the sea. Pip jumped up again, grabbing Vanessa's raincoat in her teeth and pulling until Vanessa tripped, falling against the sand.

Genny closed the distance.

"Stay down, Vanessa. It's over!" Genny panted. "We know what you did."

She scowled up at Genny as Remy pulled Vanessa up and hand-cuffed her.

"Vanessa Wollstonecraft, I am arresting you for the murder of Mitchell Collins and the attempted murder of Roisin Nobel. You do not have to say anything-"

"-That man killed my son!" Vanessa screeched as police officers swarmed the beach, coming to help them.

"-But it may harm your defence if you do not mention when questioned something which you may later rely on in court."

14

"So, Mitchell wasn't the intended victim," Genny sighed, leaning back against the wall of the living room in Foxglove Cottage, a bottle of non-alcoholic beer cradled between her palms.

"How did you figure it out?" Remy asked, sinking back next to her and swigging on his bottle of beer.

The cottage was done, although she still hadn't gotten her furniture out of storage. She had asked the Beechams to let her stay two more nights while she got her things together.

And the case was closed, with the police finding the gun and statue hidden at Vanessa's mother's house. Mitchell's body had been released and the family had been able to hold a funeral for him, attended by the whole community, mourning the tragic and unnecessary death of one of their own.

"I knew something about it wasn't right," Genny explained. "But it wasn't just the motive that was wrong, it was the person. As soon as I realised Vanessa had to be the killer, I knew it was Sandy who was her intended victim. It made sense – Mitchell had been facing away from her, in a similar jacket to Sandy, the same age, the same salt and pepper hair. She thought she had done it, until she saw the body. Then she panicked, presumably trying to frame the protestors by splashing Mitchell with the red paint. She was one of the people that Patty had in her ledger – she had bought that exact paint for her art projects."

"You did well to put it all together," Remy smiled, clinking his beer with hers.

"You are the DI, I just helped," she reminded him. "Sandy is going to make amends to the victims' families with a memorial bench in their names on the clifftop," she added. "Perhaps the gesture is too little, too late, but he's trying. His life is ravaged by guilt."

"It was a sad case all round," Remy nodded. "Mitchell was in the wrong place at the wrong time. And now Vanessa, already tortured by the death of her son will have to spend the rest of her life in prison."

"She mistook revenge for justice," Genny shrugged, "It's a hard line."

"Genny, you really need to get some sleep," DS Hutton had insisted. "Perhaps it was Harley Monan who was driving the car that hit your sister, but we can't prove it. You need to let it go."

"Could you let it go?" Genny had spat back, grief boiling over into rage. "This man killed my sister! I can't let that go."

"You're going too far," DS Hutton had sighed. "I'm worried that you're tipping over the line from serving justice to taking revenge. It isn't healthy."

"Are you okay?" Remy asked, seeing Genny lost in thought again.

"It's time I told you about why I retired from the police," Genny said, emotion catching in her throat. "My sister was killed in a hit and run."

She swallowed, waiting for his reaction. Waiting for the pity and sickly-sweet compassion to hit her. That was how people always reacted, and it was too much to bear. She steeled herself.

"Oh, wow, Genny, I'm so sorry," Remy said, inching close to her on the floor.

"Thanks," she nodded slowly.

But rather than that crushing pity she usually found in other people, she saw something else in the way Remy looked at her. He dealt with bereaved people all the time. He knew not to simper and tell her how awful it is. He knew not to say that she was in a better place, or that she was smiling down on them. He got it.

"How did it happen?" He asked.

No one ever asked that. They were scared of hurting her. But what they didn't realise that it already hurt anyway, talking about it didn't make it any worse.

"She was drunk, leaving my place after a fun evening of laughter and wine. She insisted that she could get home on her own, but being the big sister, I tried to walk her home. She was just waving to me when she stepped out and…" Genny trailed off, but Remy waited for her to find the words, not pushing her to answer. "I became obsessed with finding the driver. I refused to take other cases until I had solved my sister's case. But it really doesn't work like that. I couldn't eat, sleep or relax. I lost myself."

Remy nodded, putting a hand gently on hers.

"My family and friends were worried about me," Genny explained. "I got help – therapy. But ultimately, I couldn't solve her case." That fact still tore her up. The words cut at her throat and brought tears to her eyes. "I never found the killer, and so I decided it was best to leave the police force, and eventually London."

"That's why you decided to move here?"

"Yeah," Genny nodded. "Look how that worked out," she laughed through her tears.

"And look at the good you've done," Remy said gently. "You brought justice to someone else's family. You helped me when I needed it most."

Genny nodded slowly.

"It still hurts," she admitted. "I still keep thinking that if I could just solve Annabelle's murder… but I know it doesn't work like that."

"I can see that loss in you, now that you've pointed it out," Remy revealed. He looked up to the ceiling with a sigh. "I think it informs the way you operate."

"Is that a bad thing?" Genny asked tentatively. "I worry that... I'm closed off now."

"No, no, not at all," he answered quickly. "I think it was that attention to loss and pain that made you so vital in this case. You saw the reality of Jake's grief, of Sandy's guilt. Your sister's passing was an awful tragedy, but rather than bury it, you've let it become part of you. It's made you more sensitive to that deep pain in other people."

Genny blinked at him haltingly.

"Wow..." she said. "None of my therapists put it quite like that."

He swigged his beer and smirked at her.

"None of your therapists were detectives."

"True. You're right, though," she said. "Exactly the thing I was running from was the tonic. Policework, detective work... they are always going to be a part of me."

"Maybe you can find peace here, a new kind of life."

She smiled and put her head on his shoulder. She realised how intimate the gesture was a split second after she'd done it, but he didn't move away from her.

They stayed in comfortable silence for a few seconds before she added, "I think you could be right, about all of it."

15

"Thank you for everything, Tom and Bev," Genny said, pulling them each into a hug in turn. "You will have free cakes for life once the bakery is open, I promise."

"Oh, don't mention it," Bev said with a wave of her hand. "And don't think we didn't see the cheque you tried to leave us in your room. I ripped it up! We don't want your money!"

"I don't think I'll ever be able to repay you," Genny said. "You truly saved me in a sticky situation."

"Free pies as well?" Tom suggested with a cheeky wink.

"Definitely," Genny said with a smile.

Remy had offered to help her move in. She had been a little surprised by his generosity, given that the case was over. She was thrilled that he still wanted to be friends, even if they were no longer working together.

She had grown quite fond of him. The joy of solving the case had been marred by the fact that she was back to just being another islander, not working with the police. Not working on a mystery.

"Are you ready?" He called from the hire van.

They had collected her furniture from the storage depot the night before, and now finally she could put all of her belongings in her new home.

"Ready," she said, with a final grateful squeeze of Bev's arm.

"Don't be a stranger," Bev said.

"You can't get rid of me that easily, don't worry!" Genny laughed.

It only took a few hours to unload all of the furniture and boxes, although she suspected it would take her a few weeks to get everything unpacked properly.

"Have you looked at the bakery yet?" Remy asked her, leaning on a bookcase as they admired the cottage.

"Not yet," she admitted. "It's all a bit more overwhelming than I first thought."

"How so?" He asked, walking towards her. "Look at what you've achieved already. Your fresh start."

"Well, I've never run a bakery before," she replied sardonically. "It might be quite difficult."

"You don't strike me as someone who cares if things are difficult or not," he pointed out. "You'll get there. The village is going to be so excited to have a bakery again that they might even overlook a few burnt loaves and badly piped cake decorations."

"Maybe," she said with a half-smile. "But it's not detective work."

"I believe that was precisely the point, wasn't it?" He said, inching towards the side door that lead to the bakery. "Come on – let's have a look at it."

She nodded, looking around again before following him in.

The builders had done an exemplary job. Mitchell had left his stamp on the place with a handmade wooden countertop for the till. The cake fridge she had ordered would fit in next to it.

She had asked Mitchell to source second-hand tables and chairs for the dining area, as mismatched as possible to give it a homely vibe. They were stacked in the corner, but already she could picture how it would look.

She imagined fairy lights on the walls and the gentle chatter of customers. She could smell the coffee brewing and cakes baking in the back.

"It nearly destroyed me, being a detective," she said to Remy, blinking back bittersweet tears. "But I was good at it. It's hard to walk away from something you know you're good at."

"You'll be good at this too, I know it," he insisted, gesturing around. "It looks amazing."

"Yeah, Mitchell did a great job," she said with a sad smile.

"Yes, he did," Remy said. "And you never know, I might need your help on another case soon enough."

Genny wheeled around to look at him.

"Really?"

He shrugged, "Nothing yet but… we made a good team."

"Yeah, we did," she beamed, relief spreading through her.

It could be the perfect arrangement. The best of both worlds.

He smiled. "Well, then, I know where to find you if I have a case that I can't figure out."

Pick up Book Two in the series now!

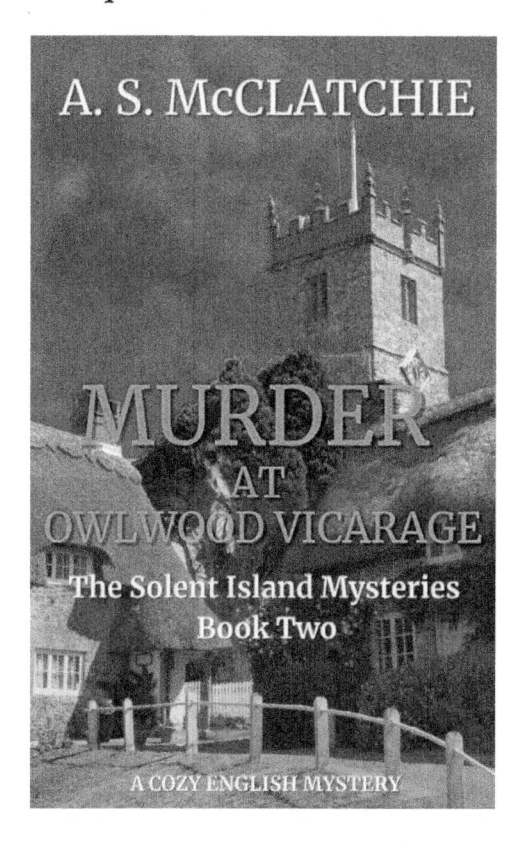

A. S. McCLATCHIE

MURDER AT OWLWOOD VICARAGE

The Solent Island Mysteries
Book Two

A COZY ENGLISH MYSTERY

About the Author

A.S. McClatchie is a cozy mystery writer from the UK, best known for her series *The Solent Island Mysteries*. When she's not re-watching episodes of *Death in Paradise* or *Midsomer Murders*, she's out walking the south Dorset coastline.

About *Murder at Solent Island Lighthouse*

This is the first cozy mystery novel in this long-running series set on the fictional Solent Island. Thank you for all of your support with this first book!

If you enjoyed this, please leave me a review on Goodreads or Amazon to help me out. Small authors like me really need the reader's help to get their books out there.
The second book will be released in December 2023!

A huge thank you to my artist Rhiannon Walters (Lunarbird Art) for the two maps at the start of this book.

Instagram:

@aprilshowerspublishing

www.aprilshowerspublishing.com

Printed in Great Britain
by Amazon